# Something Final

Sarah Dale

*Dedication*
*To the libraries: big, small, fancy and plain. And to the librarians*
*who still believe in magic. I am grateful for you all.*

Printed in the United States of America

This edition Printed, 2022

ISBN-13: 978-1-952667-99-2
AISN: 978-1-952667-98-5

If you're reading this, you've found my hidey hole. I've been keeping journals of our adventures for more than three decades now, and up until last week, I believed them to be safely hidden in my home. Now, everything has changed.

It's not that I fear they will be discovered; rather the opposite, I fear they'll be destroyed, and the record of our life's work would simply disappear.

I'm putting them here for safekeeping. I've spent enough hours in this library to know what gets tended regularly, and what gets regularly overlooked. So if you're finding this now, you must be doing a deep clean or maybe, just maybe, the City has come together with the funds for a new building, and this one is being cleared out.

Do me a favor. Do what you can to keep these safe. Tuck them back away, or move them if you need to, but don't let them be destroyed.

And if it's you they're meant for, then, good luck, my friend. You're going to need it.

Monday,
February
20, 1989

I LEANED OVER, hands on my knees, gasping for breath, my face uncomfortably close to the splotch of greenish-purple goo on the frozen ground in front of me. Moments ago, it had been some kind of crabby spider thing. Its body was about the size of Mom's sugar bowl, but it sported a dozen or so spiky dark green legs and super long antennae. This particular edition of the David, Jenny and Angie clean up weird stuff that has emerged from the Portal *from who-knows-where* wasn't the worst, but it was definitely top three in aerobic workouts. Jane

Fonda could just try to keep up.

About 200 of them had erupted from it this morning and Jen, David and I had spent the last two hours tracking them down and squishing them.

I say it was us but it was mostly Shadow and Tati who were doing the tracking. We just did the catching and the squishing.

*Ew.*

I caught my breath enough to straighten up and look around. I was on the back side of the bleachers overlooking the Wesleyan Plainsmen's football field. Tati had scared up a half dozen of the critters who hid briefly under a bush, then scattered. Jen and Shadow took off to the south, David and Tati chased after the two headed up a tree, and I got stuck with this guy.

I slowed my breath while I watched the goo slowly spread over the frozen dirt. After a minute it would merge with the icy soil and then fade entirely away. Thankfully these critters were the sort that dematerialized after we killed them. Something about their unexpected transition through the portal, Maka thought. Maybe related to the speed or the length of their journey.

We weren't always so lucky. The flying things that came out of it last week were pretty gnarly. They were sort of bat-like, black and scaly with mega-sharp claws. The only reason we were able to catch them at all was that apparently our gravity was harder to overcome than wherever they came from. Their flight was heavy and burdened.

Mr. Rakow nipped back to his car and snagged a couple of nets on long poles from his trunk, and we brought them down. Once down, though, we had to kill them – as quickly and humanely as possible, at David's insistence. He had zero tolerance for making any creature suffer a clumsy end. Creatures like that also didn't just dissolve, but had to be removed to Maka's unused horse pasture and burned.

Lots of stuff didn't even survive the journey. Those always made me feel a complicated mix of relief and sadness. I lost no sleep about the Eridani and the Walking Things, though. Those buggers took weeks to hunt down, and even after the time they spent just surviving on this alien world, they were still dangerous and tough to eliminate.

The Portal started spilling this stuff out almost two years ago, shortly after we'd solved Shelly's murder. In point of fact, it was just after Lisa explained what they'd learned about our stone necklaces that we got the first alert that something was amiss. And boy, it was some alert!

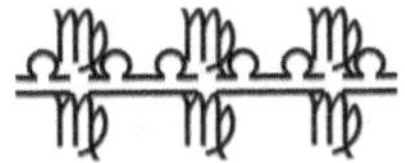

WE'D BEEN GATHERED in Lorraine's garage when Lisa offered to share with us what she and Maka had determined about the stones in our necklaces and what they meant to our abilities – Jen's prophecy, my healing, and if Mr. Rakow was to be believed, David's growing intuitive connection to the dogs.

I knew it was true because I'd seen it happen. Back then, we'd get ready to go someplace and David would cock his head one way and then the other. Tati first, and then Shadow would copy that head tilt, and immediately hop up and come to him for directions. It would even wake them up from a solid sleep, or bring them running from the far reaches of the house. No words spoken. It was pretty cool.

Lorraine had already told us that Maka and Lisa believed they'd found a connection between the missing piece of jewelry from Shelly's mom's collection and a particular meteor that was in our celestial neighborhood in the months that the three of us were born, from the Winter Solstice of 1969 to the Autumnal Equinox of 1970.

What we didn't know was that once Lisa told us all she'd learned that afternoon in Lorraine's garage, everything we'd done, everything we'd been focusing on, and everything Dad and Maka had been doing to keep the Portal safely hidden was going to undergo a radical change.

Most of the Coven witches had wandered off by then, and were chatting with Lorraine and Rakow outside. Jen, David, Jon and I had dragged the big floor pillows over to where Lisa sat knitting, with Nicole seated on the other side of her knitting basket. Nicole's elegantly long, beringed fingers rolled yarn from the opposite end of the skein into a tidy ball that, despite the forest green hue of the dye, glowed slightly blue from the magic dancing from Nicole's fingers.

We gathered around like kindergartners at storytime. Lisa beamed at us. Nicole beamed at Lisa. "It began with a series of portents in December of 1969," Lisa said. The scarf she was knitting grew longer and more colorful as she spoke.

"Portents?" Jon asked, adjusting his pillow closer to mine. I heard the door chunk closed softly as Lorraine and Rakow stepped back inside.

"It was so cold the week the twins were born," Lorraine remembered. "They only made it to 36 weeks. There was already snow on the ground, I remember that, but the day I went to the hospital, it was too cold for more snow." She accepted the lawn chair Rakow offered and they both sat down, just as keenly interested as we were to hear the story.

"Which made the unfrozen ground and the sudden appearance of full grown, blooming sunflowers all along 56th Street, all along your path, Lorraine, from home to Bryan Hospital, even more obvious," Lisa said, nodding.

"Weird!" David said, adjusting himself on his pillow to accommodate Shadow and Tati.

"Then there was the statue of the woman in the sculpture garden at Sheldon, the Art Museum on the downtown campus. What is that called? I always forget its title…"

Nicole tapped one fingernail on the side of her nose and thought. "Miller is the sculptor, something with an S…Sandy! That's it. 'Sandy In Defined Space.'"

"We saw her on a field trip last year," I remembered. "What happened to her?"

"She became magnetized" Lisa said, grinning.

"Wait, isn't she cast in bronze?" I asked, puzzled.

"Yep!" Lisa replied.

David cocked his head at me. "Let me guess, bronze is not a magnetic material?"

"Correctamundo," I replied.

"Except for about three days in December of 1969, that holds true. But, for those few days, she was. The University tried to keep it quiet, but students found out, of course, and decorated her nightly with fridge magnets. And then, on the 22nd, they all fell off into the snow."

"Double weird!" David was growing more interested by the minute.

"The third one in December was the rabbits," Lisa began.

"Oh geez, what happened to the rabbits?" I asked, hoping it was nothing awful.

"Oh yeah! I remember that," Lorraine said. "The nurses were talking about it when I was in labor. Hopping backwards, weren't they?"

"They were indeed!" Lisa exclaimed.

"And all of that happened right around the time Jen and Jon were born?" I asked.

"And ended the moment they were safely out in the world," Lisa confirmed.

"Did the same things happen around David's birth?" I asked.

"According to Rakow," Lisa nodded his direction. "At Lincoln General Hospital, the night David was born, there was a gathering of coyotes."

Mr. Rakow started rubbing his temples at this point.

I closed my own mouth which had fallen open and turned to looked at Jen. "I have so many questions," I said, my eyes wide. She nodded, her eyebrows approaching her hairline.

Lisa rolled her eyes. "Well for one thing, coyotes *don't* gather. They live in small family groups or pairs. And they certainly don't gather in a perfect circle around a hospital in south Lincoln!"

"And Mr. Rakow knows about this because…?" Jen asked pointedly.

"Because he saw it," Lisa confirmed, nodding happily.

"And you were at the hospital the night I was born, because…?" David looked straight at Rakow. His voice was a little tight. Lisa suddenly realized what was up and bit her lip. Nicole lay a comforting hand on Lisa's knee. We all waited for the other shoe to drop.

"Because I took your mom to the hospital that

night," Mr. Rakow said calmly, meeting David's eyes.

Jaws dropped all around as we processed this tidbit.

"You never told me that. You never even told me you were friends with Mom back then," David said, his voice betraying a little tension. He seemed willing to give Mr. Rakow the benefit of the doubt, that somehow there would be some kind of totally obvious explanation for not mentioning it, but I could tell he was shook up. Mr. Rakow could be kind of secretive, but he and David had grown so close, especially since both Donna and Shelly had died, it seemed odd that this detail had remained buried.

Mr. Rakow sighed. He eyed the four of us. "Lincoln is a small town, *grunts*." That was his name for us when explaining something he felt we should already know. It was generally followed by some unpopular order, often involving running a mile or lots and lots of pushups. "We went to school together, until Donna dropped out, anyway," Rakow said, then paused, thinking back.

"You guys were friends in high school?" I asked, hoping he'd continue.

"Yep. We all grew up right around here. Went to Mickle and Northeast together."

Jen's eyes were laser focused on Mr. Rakow. "We *all*?" she asked pointedly.

Mr. Rakow sighed and glanced at Lisa, who smiled at him encouragingly, if a little nervously. "Guess it's ancient history day," he muttered.

I settled myself cross-legged on my big pillow and flipped open a new page of my notebook. I had been working with Lorraine, developing a spell that allowed me to write hands-free. It wasn't perfect yet, sometimes it was pretty tough to decipher, but I was getting better. I held out both hands, ignited the spell with a quiet,

*Cerebrum Scribe,* and words began appearing on the page in bright blue ink, as quickly as I could think them.

"Donna was part of a group of kids I hung out with, all through school," Mr. Rakow began. "Neighborhood kids. You know, we weren't a *bad* group, but none of us was what you'd call, 'college-bound' *or* 'upwardly mo-bile. '" He included mildly sarcastic air quotes here for em-phasis.

"We all had jobs back then, mostly because our folks didn't have any scratch to spare. They all worked at hot, loud jobs just to keep roofs over our heads. We weren't the sort of kids who got an allowance."

While he spoke, Mr. Rakow rose from his lawn chair and paced a bit before coming to rest, leaning against the door jamb, staring at the knob as though he was forcing himself to stay put and not attempt escape.

Mr. Rakow wasn't old back then, even though he sort of looked it. His brown hair was indiscriminately shot with gray. I'm not sure who cut his hair, but I envi-sioned a tiny old barbershop on some side street with one barber chair and a cracked vinyl sofa along the wall, fre-quented by grizzled old dudes talking about the Corn-huskers or politics or hog futures. His skin was a shade of perma-tan more associated with sun damage than vibrant good health.

Mr. Rakow's energy was often low key, but never in a lazy way. On the contrary, he was constantly on the move, but always in a measured, experienced way. No step he trod was new – his feet had been everywhere be-fore. In any environment I'd ever seen him, he always seemed at ease, well prepared, entirely comfortable.

He was like that when he fought, too. I'd had a front-row seat to his one-on-one battle energy more than once over the past few years, but it was that very first time that was seared into my brain. It was watching him battle the Ghost of Charlie Starkweather in the broad hallway in front of the library at my junior high on Halloween.

My energy in that moment had been a torrent of barely controlled fear and outrage. The only thing holding me in check that day was my connection to Jen and David. Because of the connection of our necklaces, they shared my pool of energy. I never had to face anything totally alone.

But Mr. Rakow *was* alone, and it was cool. It fit him perfectly to be self-contained. He seemed very much at peace with and wholly connected to himself. I kinda wanted to be Mr. Rakow when I grew up.

I took a good look at him now, leaning against the doorframe, a half empty PBR longneck caught between the knuckles of his pointer and middle fingers on the left hand. He wore a faded blue Frank Zappa '84 t-shirt tucked into gray/green cargo pants.

He also wore authentic Mexican huaraches, a gift Jules brought him from her last trip south. A gift which had Jen and I all aflutter for about five minutes until Jules dashed our romantic hopes for the two of them by announcing a new long-distance romance with Alejandro, a junior Professor of Archaeology at UNAM in Mexico City. He was supervising a dig. She was hiking nearby. They met in a cantina, bonded over carbon-dating Yaxchilan artifacts and she was already planning a return visit.

Regardless, the huaraches were a solid second option to his shoe collection, which heretofore had consisted of exactly one pair of rugged hiking boots. They suited him. Mr. Rakow was variously cool, badass, unflinchingly loyal and so chill he was almost boring. This conversation, however, had him rattled.

I knew he and Donna had lived next door to one another ever since I'd first met David in kindergarten. I never thought to wonder if he and Donna had known each other before that. Then I felt dumb for not wondering.

*Note to self: Wonder about more things.*

"Donna was a couple years younger than me," Rakow said. "Our moms were friends from the neighborhood. Her mom knew she was a handful and at different times, they both asked me to kind of, look out for her."

"Mom was a handful?" David asked, a trace of defensiveness in his tone despite all she'd put him through. Your mom is still your mom, I guess. No matter what.

"In a lot of ways," interrupted Lorraine, grinning broadly, "she was legendary." We all turned to her, surprised. "David, your mom was fearless! There was no car too fast, no adventure too crazy, no dare she wouldn't take on. Obviously, I don't recommend her careless relationship with booze, that can get the best of anybody. But her boldness and audacity were the stuff of neighborhood legend. She was a big deal to us younger girls."

David smiled at that, and then frowned.

Lorraine stood and walked over to the table that still contained a cooler of ice and drinks, and a jug of mostly melted ice and a little tea. She poured herself a cup. On the way, she dropped a kiss on the top of David's head. "She was a complicated person, your mom, but she was also fierce and fabulous."

"Tell about the night David was born, Mr. Rakow." Jen said gently.

Mr. Rakow faced David directly and began to speak in a calm, earnest tone. "We worked together, bud, all during the time she was pregnant with you. I got the job as a kitchen manager at the Misty's in Havelock after I graduated. She was working as a dishwasher. When she couldn't cover up the pregnancy any more, she dropped out of school."

I mentally ground my teeth at that. She, and David could have been so much better off later if she'd been able to stay in school. Stupid societal norms. I quickly shushed my inner fairness warrior and tuned back into Mr. Rakow.

"I talked the General Manager into giving her a couple extra breaks during shifts if she needed them, but otherwise not freaking out about having a pregnant teenage dishwasher." He sipped his beer and wiped his mouth with the back of his hand before he continued.

"She worked right up to the night you were born. She motioned me over to where she was taking a break. I remember she was sitting in the broken chair we'd drug over there – before that the only thing to sit on in that shitty little corner of the back room was a milk carton and an upside-down bucket. We made shims out of a pallet and got it steady enough for her to sit on.

"She looked up at me, her face all steamy and red from the heat of the dishwasher. She goes, 'Shit, Rakow, it's starting and my damn car has a flat. I walked to work today, could you…?' I'd already planned on doing it, to be honest. Her car was busted more often than it worked. Her mom had passed away from cancer a few months before that, back around Christmas, and her dad still had his head buried in the blues and whiskey. He wasn't no help."

"What about *my* dad? Was he around back then? Did you know him too?" David asked, his voice tight with complicated feelings.

Mr. Rakow's lips tightened. "By then, buddy, he'd already taken off," Mr. Rakow said.

"But, you knew him?" David asked quietly.

"Yeah, I knew him." There was a wealth of feeling in that statement that I could only guess at. Had they been friends? Enemies? Rivals? Whatever it was, it seemed to have ended badly. I filled a whole notebook page with question marks and exclamation points.

David took a deep breath and let it out slowly. Both dogs raised their heads. Shadow pawed at his left leg and Tati butted at his right hand. He petted her, stiffly at first, but then more naturally. She licked his fingers. David shook his head and said gruffly, "Whatever. Let's hear about the coyotes, since that's what we're talking about."

"Sure, yeah." Mr. Rakow sounded relieved. "We can talk about the other stuff later."

"Can't wait," David muttered. Tati butted at his hand again and he resumed scratching behind her ears.

"Anyway," said Mr. Rakow, clearing his throat, "we bailed out of work. Boss was pissed, but we were through the evening rush, anyway. By the time we got to the hospital it was dusk, not totally dark. I saw them first as we drove up the entryway to the ER. I saw their eyes glowing in my headlights when I rounded that curve off South Street. One set of eyes, then two or three more, all the way up to the hospital.

"Once we got upstairs in a room, I looked out the window and I could see them out there, sitting, watching the hospital. It was wild."

"Then what happened?" I asked, rapt.

"Then, Donna's labor kicked in hard core and she started screaming at me to get out, so I did," replied Mr. Rakow, sounding equal parts sheepish and relieved.

"You were born a little later that night. I got to see you a few times before I had to leave." Mr. Rakow drained his bottle and walked over to where Lorraine kept the glass for recycling.

"That's right, you left that summer, didn't you?" Lorraine asked.

"Left for?" Jen asked.

"I was drafted that summer," said Mr. Rakow. "I spent the next two years trying not to do anything stupid that would get me killed in Vietnam.

"You were in for longer than two years, though, weren't you?" I asked.

"I was. They took two, and I gave them another eight of my own damfool free will. Came back to Lincoln when my mom got laid up and ended up staying."

"Your mom was a blessing to everyone she ever met, Rakow," Lorraine said softly. He gave her a sad smile in return.

"So," I said, eyeing my notes. "Jen and Jon got backwards hopping bunnies, magnetized artwork, and sunflowers in the snow. David's day was marked by a gathering of coyotes. How about me?" I looked up at Lisa, my curiosity burning.

"I had to do some real digging to figure that out, Angie," Lisa replied. "In fact, Jules found the first clue."

"What did Jules find?" Jon asked. He was just as eager as I was to hear.

Lisa grinned at the two of us and set her knitting down in her lap. "One of her travel friends belongs to a birding club. Turns out, their club president was out and about near St. Elizabeth Hospital that afternoon and spotted a sandhill crane dancing near the koi pond on the hospital grounds."

"A sandhill crane, in town?" I asked. Sandhill cranes, as their names suggest, are most often spotted in and around the Sandhills in western Nebraska, several hours drive west of Lincoln. Their spring migration is a big tourist draw for the state. Their fall migration is less spectacular because unlike in the spring when they stop all along the Platte River and feed in the surrounding fields, in the fall, they go more directly south, sometimes bypassing Nebraska altogether. They were almost never around Lincoln, and for sure not right in town.

"Dancing?" David asked. "Isn't that a mating thing?"

"It is," Lisa replied, "but not exclusively. They're seen dancing quite often. They're not anywhere near Nebraska that early in the fall, however. But, even odder than any of those things, was its color."

"They're usually, like, grey or brown, right?" Jen asked. "What color was this one?"

"White. Pure white. *Leucistic* is the term Jules used." She enunciated the scientific term carefully.

The word appeared in my notebook as *Lou Cist Ick*. Yikes, I was going to have to check the spelling on that one. "Well, that's curious," I said contemplatively, trying not to sound disappointed. Gathering of coyotes, magnetic copper artwork and paths of sunflowers seemed pretty cool by comparison.

"That's not all of it, but this next bit is based on hospital gossip. The facts themselves are part of peoples' private medical records, so of course, nothing we can look at. But people noticed what happened, and people talk." Lisa said, her face alight with excitement.

"What is it?" Lorraine asked excitedly. "What's the gossip?"

"According to my sources, nobody died at the hospital that day," she said, smiling broadly.

Rakow frowned. "I can't help hoping that in a city this size, a day with nobody dying in one modern hospital isn't totally unheard of?"

"It's less common than you think, and what makes it

even more unusual, is that it continued. There were no deaths recorded at St. Elizabeth hospital for fully three weeks starting in September of 1970. And it gets even better than that!" She beamed at me. Jon's hand was warm on my back.

"Every single person who was in the hospital that day experienced significant healing. My nurse friend, Sam, said it was first noticed in the ER. A car accident with three victims, two in surgery, all pulled through. Then, the ER started emptying out. Folks who'd showed up with high fevers, irregular heartbeats, even one drug overdose. People just, got better.

"Bones that had been X-rayed and declared fractured showed several weeks' worth of healing in a few hours. And get this. Three different people who were there with stage four cancers spontaneously went into complete re-mission. Throughout the hospital, people were checking themselves out, happily confused and relieved, calling it a miracle."

Lisa looked around at us. Jen had scooted her pillow a little closer to Lorraine's lawn chair. She sat with her head cocked, deep in thought. Lorraine's eyes were starshine bright, her smile beatific. David and Rakow's uncomfortable tension, incited by Rakow's revelations about David's dad, had evaporated. They both looked amazed.

Jon, by now leaning shoulder to shoulder with me on the same pillow, puffed his chest out a little and said, "That's my girlfriend!"

"Um, zoinks?" I offered sheepishly. "I mean, obvi-ously that sits on my mom's shoulders, being a Master Healer and all, but wow! Just wow!"

"And," Lisa continued, still grinning excitedly, "at all three locations on each of the three nights, meteor

showers were reported by the local news. From my research, I've been able to not only determine that meteoric
objects fell from the sky onto the hospital grounds on the
specific days that each of you kids was born, but," she
paused here and rather dramatically thrust her hand deep
into her yarn bag. Her face looked like my mom's always
did on Christmas mornings when she was super happy
and anticipating how Mal and I were going to love whatever she got us.

"I have obtained samples from each meteor shower!"
She held out the box she'd had secreted in her yarn bag.
It was rectangular and looked and smelled like it had once
held fancy scented soaps. She drew off the lid. Carefully
nestled in each of the three little sections that had once
held a milled Parisian moisturizing bar, was a more or less
golf ball-sized chunk of blackened space rock.

"Those things fell from space on the days we were
born?" David asked, peering at them.

They *looked* alien to me, space-black and cold.
"Which is which?" I asked.

"Turn them over." Jon's voce was quiet, his tone ex-
pectantly curious.

David, being closest, looked to Lisa for permission.
She grinned over at Jon and held the box out within David's easy reach.

He flipped the first stone over and from either side
of me, Jen and Jon simultaneously exclaimed, "Thar she
blows!"

On this side, the stone had cracked open to expose a
deep red crystalline center, identical to the stone in Jen's
necklace. David flipped the second stone and exposed its
cracked open side; this one was David's green. I could
feel the warmth from my blue stone necklace, glowing
against my collarbone before David even turned the third

space rock over.

The moment he did so, my necklace dimmed briefly and then danced with light. I reached out intuitively for Jen's hand and found it reaching for mine. David's warm, strong hand gripped my other wrist and I clasped his back.

The voices around us faded to a low murmur. Hinkiness was very clearly afoot.

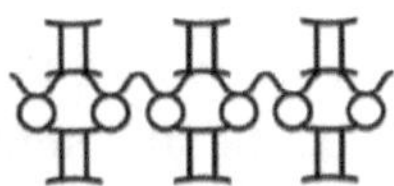

IT WAS A vision. A seriously bitchin' vision. Seriously. With lights and surround sound and 360-degree views. I wondered if it was Jen's vision and we were all sharing it, or if it was something coming from the parental meteor rocks to our necklaces. Then I told myself to shut up and pay attention.

We very realistically appeared to be in outer space. I checked in with my lungs to make sure this was, in fact, just a vision and not another portal like the enchanted Rubik's cube that transported us off planet last time. Breathe in, breathe out. Okay, so far so good – no freaky dying in the vacuum of space today. Just, like, totally hanging out, sort of motionless, holding hands with my BFFs in the vastness of space.

"Well, this is fun," David quipped in my head. "Where are we?"

*I could hear him in my head in this vision. Cool.*

"Still in our own solar system," I replied, looking around carefully. "If I'm right, we're looking at Mars, which would mean …" I cast my eyes around toward the distant brightness of the Sun and gasped in delight. "There's Earth! Look, you guys, look!"

There she was, our home planet floating gracefully in the darkness, lit by the rays of our brilliant Sun. I'd seen the amazing picture of the Earth taken by the astronaut on Apollo 8, what's his name, Anders, back in December of 1969 and been just as enchanted by it as every other Earthling. But this was years before the Hubble telescope or any of the other high-resolution photos we have today. And we were *there*.

"Oh, wow," said Jen, the awe evident in her tone.

David had no words, he just stared.

We gazed silently at the beautiful, delicate blue marble hanging there in the enormous darkness. I don't know about Jen and David, but I could have happily stayed just like that for hours, staring in fascinated awe. But there was no time. No time before we were all accosted by an intense buzzing sound that filled our heads.

I clapped my hands to my ears, but that helped not at all since the sound, like our voices, was inside my head. Then the sound changed from buzzing to a clicking, and then to a sound like wind in the trees, and then again to something that sounded vaguely like music. The notion of a radio changing stations, trying to tune into the correct signal occurred to me.

"Hello?" I asked, surprising myself. "Hello?"

*HELLO?* A distant, echoey voice replied.

"Erk," I replied, cleverly.

"Whoa," intoned David.

The star-studded blackness of space grew slightly more distant and a rocky surface appeared underfoot. I took in jagged, rocky surfaces, some waist-high, others as tall as a water tower, their peaks ice-tipped.

"Look," whispered Jen. I turned toward the sound of

her voice in my head and saw more of the same black stone but it wasn't raw or jagged. These wall-sized sections had been engraved with pristine lines onto polished surfaces that gleamed.

"What the?" David exclaimed.

"Isn't that writing?" Jen asked.

I peered at the characters carved into the stone and gasped. "We've seen these glyphs before!" Back in the ancient ruins with Maka and Malinowski!" I recognized it from that long hallway we'd taken on the way to the armory on our way to rescue Barb and Alesta.

*HELLO ANGIE. HELLO DAVID AND JENNY – AND THE BROTHER AND FRIEND JON WHO IS ALWAYS NEARBY. GREETINGS AND WELCOME.*

The voice came from nowhere and everywhere.

"Who are you?" I asked. "What is this place?"

*The voice spoke again with a slightly mechanical accent, I AM CALLED CALLEAN, AND THIS PLACE IS ME.*

I instinctively jumped, pulling first one foot and then the other up off the surface before remembering that this was a vision, and anyway, my tennies probably wouldn't hurt a creature made (*mostly?*) of space rock.

"Are you from the between place?" I asked. "Where Maka brought us to help rescue Barb and Alesta?"

*YES AND NO, YOUNG SCHOLAR. THAT PLACE IS ONE WHERE MY RACE ONCE LIVED, BUT THAT WAS AGES AGO. MY HOME PLANET IS OLDER BY LIGHT YEARS OF MAGNITUDE THAN ANY OF THE PLANETS ALIVE TODAY.*

I opened my mouth to ask another question and was beaten to the punch by Jen.

"You have something important you want to tell us, and something else you do not wish to tell us," Jen said.

I could tell by the tone of her voice that she was fully tapped into her prophetic sense as she spoke.

*AS ALWAYS, YOU SPEAK TRUTH, PROPHET.* The voice sounded only vaguely mechanical, and not creepy like HAL in "2001: A Space Odyssey." In fact, it sounded sort of nice.

*MY MISSION IS TO TRAVEL,* Callean began, sounding now like he was reading from a cue card, or an official report. *TO LOCATIONS WHERE THE PORTAL HAS OPENED AND IDENTIFY LIKELY CANDIDATES WHOSE NATIVE ABILITIES CAN BE ENHANCED WITH THE TECHNOLOGY MY KIND HAVE DEVISED TO PROTECT IT.*

"And you identified us," David asked, "as likely candidates?"

*USING THE DATA I'VE GATHERED SINCE I ENTERED YOUR SOLAR SYSTEM 347 YEARS AGO, I IDENTIFIED THE EXPLORER, MAKA; THE SENSEI, RAKOW; THE GUARDIAN AND THE HEALER, YOUR PARENTS, SCHOLAR; AND, OF COURSE, YOU THREE. EACH OF YOU HAS AN ENERGY SIGNATURE THAT MY KIN AND I, HAVE LEARNED TO SEARCH FOR NEAR THE FOCUS POINTS. WE HAVE LEARNED THAT BEINGS WITH THAT SIGNATURE ARE BEST ABLE TO USE THE TOOLS I PROVIDED EACH OF YOU WITH. THE TOOLS YOU'D NEED TO FULFILL THE TASK OF PROTECTING THE PORTAL, UNTIL ITS INEVITABLE COLLAPSE.*

"Our necklaces," I murmured. "They're not *just* stone."

*CORRECT, SCHOLAR.* Callean said. *YOUR NECKLACES ARE MADE OF THE SAME MATERIAL FROM WHICH THIS BODY IS MADE –*

*LIVING STONE. ORGANIC MATERIAL INTRINSI-CALLY BOUND UP WITH MACHINE INTELLI-GENCE. THEY ALLOW YOU TO CONNECT MORE FULLY TO THE ABILITIES YOU ALREADY POS-SESS.*

*Oh, wow. That was, wow.* My usual million questions bubbled up into my throat.

"The Portal," Jen urged him, and me, patiently.

*THE PORTAL ON EARTH IS BEGINNING TO CLOSE. THIS WILL BE A CRITICAL TIME FOR YOU AND FOR THE GUARDIAN.*

"How so?" David asked.

*DURING THIS PROCESS, THE PORTAL WILL BE UNSTABLE. HERE, ALLOW ME TO SHOW YOU…*

In the space of a heartbeat, the glyphs covering one of the stone structures lit up like an instrument panel and then morphed into a theater-sized screen. A picture materialized and I squinted to wrap my brain around what it was showing us.

It was an aerial view, from maybe a second or third floor height, of a town square, I thought. The general grouping of buildings around one taller one fit that pattern anyway, but everything else was strange.

The buildings were more rounded than squared, and seemed to be constructed of rolled tubes of the same sort of orange-colored, sandy soil that made up the flat land here as well as the nearby hills. Scrubby vegetation and a few low, twisted trees dotted the hills. Similar plants had been decoratively situated around the buildings – a few of which were bushes covered with an explosion of striking, blood-red blooms.

The curved walls of the structures were adorned with bright, bold patterns that sort of reminded me of the pottery we'd seen on our trip to Santa Fe last summer. Instead of any recognizable bird or sun imagery, though, I saw representations of six-legged creatures with ferocious looking teeth, and lots of images of something bright blue and snaky.

Folks were abroad. I couldn't see any faces or details under the full robes they wore, ostensibly as protection from the blinding double suns in the sky.

"Where is this?" David asked. "What are we seeing?"

*THIS IS THE FORMER HOME OF MAKA'S STUDENT, MALINOWSKI. IT WAS MANY GENERATIONS BACK WHEN THE PORTAL ON THAT MOON WAS JUST BEGINNING TO DESTABILIZE. WATCH, CHILDREN.*

We watched.

Everything seemed normal, folks moving about, doing their thing. Then without any warning I could detect, a fountain of water sputtered to life from one side of a building I thought may have been a market, judging by the bags hanging off peoples' arms as they exited. It looked like a giant, black hose gone mad, but one end was wide open and the other end was a tiny pinprick.

First, people ran out of that building, shouting. Then folks started pouring out of nearby buildings to see what was up. The fountain of water from the wide open end wasn't slowing down – in fact it was getting bigger. It flailed madly. The water spread out in front of the store and ran downhill, towards our viewpoint. The flow of water continued to increase in volume until it seemed actual waves were erupting out of nowhere. A dank, fishy smell rose from it.

Folks scurried away, running away from us and uphill to our left, where I could see a tall, formal-looking compound of buildings, even more brightly and beautifully decorated than the town square. The water soaked into the dry ground fast, but there was more coming every second, and then it wasn't just water. Creatures began coming out too.

Fishy things appeared first, maybe the size of my hand and bright blue. They zoomed out on the wave of water from nowhere, wriggling and glinting in the ferocious sunshine, only to be dashed to the sandy ground to flop and expire helplessly as their protective watery atmosphere was suddenly replaced by hot dry sand and burning sunlight.

A school of larger swimmers came next. This group silver and antennaed, flopping and gasping as they hit the ground in a growing swath as the water fanned out downhill and was absorbed into the stony ground of Malinowski's moon.

Then something approximately hippo-sized with both fins and legs, and lots and lots of teeth appeared. Whatever it was, it didn't immediately expire like the fish had when it hit the air. Instead, it gave itself a good shake, took a look around and caught the movement of three people dashing away from a building downstream and took off after them, teeth bared, a feral, ferocious look in its whirling purple eyes. People screamed.

I felt David's attempt to run, to barrel headlong into the fray, but we were formless – just along for the ride. The picture dissolved and we found ourselves back on Callean's stony surface.

"What was that thing?"

"Where did it come from?" Jen's question and mine tumbled over one another. David was silent and tense, a coiled spring.

*SCHOLAR,* Callean said pointedly. *YOU ARE FAMILIAR, I BELIEVE WITH THE EINSTEIN-ROSEN*

*BRIDGE THEORY?*

I gulped. Okay, pop quiz time. "Sort of? It describes the possibility of a stable bridge, a wormhole, from one point to another in space time. But it's only a theory, they've never been documented. Some people even think they're not bridges, but protrusions from a fourth dimension that we're unable to fully see or comprehend." I felt David and Jen's curious looks.

"I found out about them when we came back from the Between place. But, Maka said she didn't know for sure if that's what the portal was."

*EXACTLY* Callean responded. *AND, MAKA IS CORRECT. WHAT YOUR PHYSICISTS HAVE THEORIZED IS PARTIALLY TRUE. WORMHOLES CAN EXIST. IN A NATURRALLY OCURRING STATE THEY ARE, AS THEORIZED, UNSABLE. ITS' ONLY WITH THE ADDITION OF A SPECIFIC TYPE OF MATTER THAT THEY CAN BE PARTIALLY STABILAZED, AND EVEN THEN, THEY REMAIN IRREGULAR AND ARE SUBJECT TO UNPREDICTABLE DECAY.*

"The addition of a specific type of matter – something not naturally occurring," I said slowly. "Do you mean, someone or something is manipulating it?"

*SOMETHING IS,* Callean replied, *MANIPULATING NATURALLY OCCURRING WORMHOLES BY INSERTING THE MATTER OF THE PLACE THE PILGRIMS CALL PARADISE. THE EXOTIC MATTER SURROUNDING THAT PLACE IS BEING SEEDED OUT INTO THE UNIVERSE IN AN ATTEMPT TO DRAW MATTER BACK INTO ITSELF.*

*Oh, crap.*

"Back into the giant gaping maw of a black hole the fool Pilgrims call *Paradise*." I said dryly. "And if it succeeds, the balance of matter in the universe is irrevocably tilted and life as we know it would cease to exist." Then I paused, pushing down my irritation and snark and trying to process this new information. "But they don't stay stable, so how does that work, exactly?"

*WHEN THE WORMHOLES DESTABILIZE, OFTEN ONE SIDE OR THE OTHER BEGINS TO FLAIL AROUND, LIKE A, Callean paused, LIKE A FIREHOSE ON YOUR PLANET, CONNECTED ON ONE SIDE TO ITS SOURCE, BUT ON THE OTHER SIDE, DANGEROUSLY UNCONTROLLED.*

"And when that happens, a bridge to one place becomes a bridge to someplace else?" I asked.

"Like, the bottom of an ocean," Jen said with surety.

*YES, AS WE JUST SAW. Callean's voice sounded eerily cheerful about this. OR IT COULD BE THE INSIDE OF A VOLCANO, OR A HYDROGEN CLOUD, OR QUITE OFTEN, AN EMPTY POCKET OF SPACE! THERE'S SIMPLY NO PREDICTING WHERE AN UNTETHERED BRIDGE MAY LAND.*

"So then, whatever is on the other side gets transported through?" David asked.

*WITH SOMETIMES DISATEROUS RESULTS,* Callean confirmed.

"And you're telling us this now," Jen said, "because *our* Portal is becoming unstable."

*YES. Callean confirmed.*

"Crap!" I muttered.

"Oh boy," said Jen.

"Cool!" exclaimed David. "And it's our job to protect everybody from whatever may come out of our portal?" David asked. I pictured him in my mind's eye, gearing up for a fight.

*YES, BUT ALSO TO PROHIBIT WHAT MIGHT*

GO INTO IT – OR TRY TO.

"Because the Pilgrims might know this is their last chance at this portal, and they'd be desperate?" I mused.

*YES,* he hesitated for the space of a breath before continuing. *AND BECAUSE BY MY CALCULA-TIONS, ONE OF YOU WILL LIKELY NOT SURIVE TO SEE THE PORTAL CLOSE.*

"What?" I exclaimed.

"Who?" David cried.

"Figured," Jen muttered.

Callean's voice tightened, as if our host had a weapon aimed at him. *IF I COULD PROVIDE YOU ANY MORE DETAILS WITHOUT MAKING THE ODDS WORSE FOR YOU, I WOULD.*

"What!" David shouted. "You're not going to tell us any more than that?"

*IT'S POSSIBLE I'VE ALREADY SAID TOO MUCH, he said.* Then in a rush, he continued, *TRUST YOUR INSIGHTS, PROPHET. TRUST YOUR WIS-DOM, SCHOLAR. TRUST YOUR INSTINCTS, WAR-RIOR. TRUST ONE ANOTHER – AND GOOD LUCK, CHILDREN.*

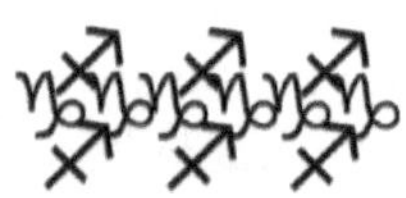

WE STARTLED AWAKE, still standing in a triangle in Lorraine's garage, hands clasped. Jon stood behind me, one hand on my shoulder, his other on Jen's. Mr. Rakow stood behind David, one hand on his shoulder, the other holding the cordless phone.

Jen's head snapped around; her eyes trained on Mr.

Rakow.

"The Portal?" she asked.

He jerked his head in the affirmative. "Guardian says we got big trouble. Gear up, grunts. We have work to do."

That day began our nearly two-year adventure with a destabilizing Portal.

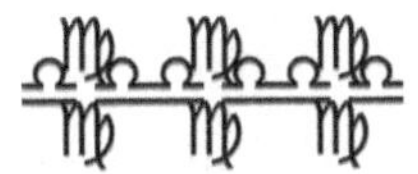

## STILL MONDAY, FEBRUARY 20th 1989
*Still behind the bleachers on Wesleyan campus. Still cold.*

I spotted Jen and Shadow jogging my direction and I let loose a sigh of relief. The sky was darkening and it was starting to look like snow.

"All clear?" I called hopefully.

"All clear!" Jen sang back. I saw David, Tati and Mr. Rakow trudging our way and waved. A loud honk sounded from the parking lot. I turned and saw Lorraine and Jon exiting Lorraine's new (used) Plymouth Volaré. I marveled at how she kept her cars so clean, even in crappy weather. Must have been magic.

Also magical was the sight of my extremely cute boyfriend carrying a thermos jug of what was, if we were lucky, Lorraine's legendary hot chocolate. She was pulling a stack of insulated coffee cups out of the back seat.

I gave Jen a hopeful look. "What d'ya think?"

"Let's go see!" she grinned. We took off towards them at a jog, David and Mr. Rakow hot on our heels.

I was surprised to see my folks pull in a few minutes

later and park next to Lorraine until I reminded myself that everyone had the day off for the President's Day holiday. I was grateful. It had made the afternoon's activities far easier than if the campus had been swarming with students.

"Hi Alden, Elizabeth. Thanks for coming on such short notice," Lorraine said, extracting a second thermos of hot chocolate from the car and pouring for my parents.

"What's up?" asked David.

"Yeah, why the impromptu staff meeting?" I asked, handing full cups off from Lorraine to my mom and dad.

"Well," Lorraine began carefully. "I just got some interesting news. David, this pertains to all of us, but specifically you." David perked up.

"Back when we started the paperwork to officially adopt David," she said, glancing around at the rest of us. "The State required us to attempt to make contact with any of his family members who might choose to exert custodial rights after Donna's death."

David nodded, reaching for more cocoa. "Right, and the only response was from the great aunt in the nursing home, Gladys, right?"

"Right. Well, one more has turned up."

"Who?" Rakow asked flatly.

Lorraine sighed and went to stand closer to David. I glanced at my folks who looked compassionately concerned. Whatever this was, they evidently already knew about it.

"You know the State wanted to know anything we had about your dad, so we gave it to them. It wasn't much. Mike doesn't have family in Lincoln anymore. He moved here with his mom when he was in ninth or tenth grade, right Rakow?

"Ninth," he replied tersely. "They moved here from South Dakota. Last I knew of his mom, she'd hooked up with some biker and they were back in South Dakota – out west, near Deadwood or Sturgis someplace."

"Yes. They looked for her, but she'd passed away. Her husband had an old address for Mike that he gave the investigators. They attempted to contact him, but didn't make any progress." She cleared her throat. "I got the address from them, and sent a postcard, thinking he might respond to somebody he actually knew as opposed to some official looking thing from the State. He was always kind of anti-establishment, wasn't he, Rakow?"

"He was that," Mr. Rakow responded dryly.

"But, did he? Did he respond to you?" David asked. His voice sounded tight. Rakow put a hand on his shoulder.

"Yes," Lorraine nodded. "He did."

"What did he say?" David asked.

Lorraine fumbled in her jacket pockets for the letter. This whole situation was so loaded. I held my breath.

"What did he say?" David repeated tensely.

Lorraine pulled the folded postcard out of her hip pocket and smoothed it out. She gently offered it to him, so he could read it first.

He looked at her, and at Rakow, nervously. I felt the tiny pinprick of warmth from my stone necklace that meant the three of us were connected, in tune. I saw his shoulders relax a few millimeters and he said more calmly, "Read it, please, so we can all hear?"

Lorraine nodded and turned to face the rest of us. The postmark is from Salt Lake City on the 15th. She read Mike's words carefully. *Lorraine – got your letter. We need to talk. God, I don't know what to think right now – crazy news! As fate would have it, I'm on my way through Lincoln, headed to DC.*

*Should get to town the 25<sup>th</sup>. Will call."*

I screwed up my eyebrows. "The 25<sup>th</sup> is Saturday!"

Lorraine had gathered David under one arm. He seemed okay, maybe just a little dazed. Rakow, however, was glowering over his shoulder.

"Yes. He called about an hour ago from Denver. He said my letter had only recently made its way to him — I guess he's moved a few times since living there." She gave David's shoulders a squeeze. "Mike said if you want him to, and *only* if you want him to, he'd like to come over and talk. He says he'll be in town for several days with his friend, Jim. I have the number of the place where they're staying when they arrive."

"You don't have to talk to him, or meet him, if you don't want to, buddy." Mr. Rakow said in a carefully neutral tone."

"He's right, honey," Lorraine seconded. "And you don't have to decide right this minute if you don't want to, either. You know we'll support whatever decision you feel comfortable with."

David slung one arm around Lorraine and the other around Rakow and hugged them together with the crushing strength of an 18-year-old who's still trying to get the hang of how strong he has become. I heard Lorraine's whoosh of breath and I smiled.

"Thanks, you guys. You are the best. You're right, too. My head is kind of spinning right now, and I'm not a hundred percent sure what I want to do."

My mom stepped in just then and put a hand on David's arm. I knew she was working some subtle healing mojo so I watched her carefully. She took a beat and then began speaking in a low, peaceful tone.

"Choosing how you want to respond to this unexpected news probably seems daunting, dear boy. Please, remember to consider yourself and your own needs kindly as you do so. There's no single right path, only the ways that are more right for you in this moment. Use your instincts, and know that we all have your back."

While she spoke, I could smell waves of the lavender-tinged healing magic flowing from her. Mom wasn't a witch, like Lorraine. Her healing magic was something more organic, not organized and directed in the manner of spellwork. It was more like a sixth sense, plus a third arm.

I watched David's frown lines smooth and his color grew a bit ruddier.

"Thank you." He squeezed mom's hand.

"Rakow," he said, "If you don't mind taking the dogs back, I'd like to go with Jen and Angie for a bit – maybe grab some Runza or something before I come home and shower. I'm starving." He stared pointedly at me and then Jen, "And it has been made crystal clear to me that I don't do my best thinking on an empty stomach."

Jen and I snorted in unison.

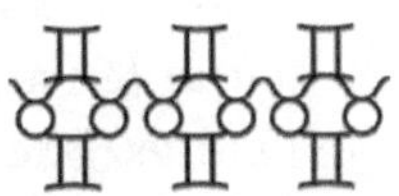

MR. RAKOW USHERED Tati and Shadow into his car. They would only leave David's side after he promised to bring them chicken tenders from Runza.

Smart dogs.

I assured my folks I'd keep them posted about any and all goings on, and they took off. Jon kissed my cheek and whispered, "I'll go with Mom. You three need some time. Bring me a cheeseburger?"

"You know I will." I returned his kiss and piled into Clint's broad front seat with Jen and David.

Jen took the long way around campus to get to the restaurant. David had opted for the middle seat, usually allocated to the one of us with the shortest legs (me). This way, his shoulders touched both of ours. I glimpsed the reflection of our glowing necklaces against the car window. It was becoming gloomier and even more overcast outside.

I pointed one of Clint's heat vents more directly at my center mass. We ordered at the drive through speaker and waited our turn in line. Runza was always busy.

Once we got our food, Jen pulled into an empty space in the parking lot. She put Clint in park but kept the engine running for the heat. David was already liberating fries from the bag. Jen and I weren't far behind. For a couple minutes there was only intense scarfing in near silence, punctuated by the crinkling of wrappers and the slurp of sodas, surrounded by the comforting aroma of salty fried goodness.

David had mowed down not one, but two Runzas, a large order of onion rings and was sucking air from the bottom of his soda cup before Jen and I were half done. He gazed longingly at Jen's fries. She locked her gaze on his, slowly and deliberately gathered the container of fries to her chest and used two elegantly long fingers tipped by long red nails to grasp the biggest one. Without releasing his gaze, she drew the fry out, poked it at him, and fast as lightning, before he could snag it, she pulled the single fry back.

He paused, prepared to ask nicely, and before he could, she proffered instead her half-full container, keeping only the largest fry for herself. "Talk," she said, holding them closer to him. He accepted the gift, and talked between bites.

"According to Rakow, back when we first talked about him knowing my dad, he said my mom never told Mike that she was pregnant. She knew he was planning to leave town and she told Rakow later that he didn't need to know. That it wouldn't help anything and she especially didn't want Mike's Mom, my Grandma Ellis, to know about it. I guess Mom really didn't like her, and couldn't stand the idea of having to tolerate her coming around.

"Rakow said he didn't agree with all that, but he figured it was her call, anyway. Then, of course, he got drafted and had pretty much no idea what was going on with Mom for a while. She wasn't much of a letter-writer, he said." He hmphed a little at that.

Jen nodded and indicated with a wave of her straw for him to continue.

"So, it sounds like the first Mike even knew about me was just recently, whenever he saw Lorraine's letter." David went on.

"Right, that must have been a surprise," I murmured around a mouthful.

"Yeah, and it's weird that like, neither one of us knew anything. I mean, of course I knew I had a dad, but mom literally never said anything about him. Nothing good, nothing bad, just nothing. Like he didn't exist."

"Did you think about him anyway? Like, what would happen if he suddenly showed up?" Jen asked. I knew there was a piece of time when we were in kindergarten and first grade when her dad didn't come around at all. She thought all sorts of crazy things about him back then, so I knew she understood how having an absent dad might feel.

"Kinda?" He paused. "I mean, not like this, but

maybe what I might say to him if I ever met him, you know?" He wiped his greasy hands on a napkin a little more ferociously than strictly necessary.

"Please tell me," Jen said in a teasingly long-suffering tone, "that the Johnny Cash song, "A Boy Named Sue" isn't the soundtrack to your imagined meeting." I caught my breath, but said nothing. If Jen was really concerned that David was going to get into a bloody fistfight with his long-lost father, she wouldn't be teasing.

Sure enough, he looked up at her and grinned. "I think we're good. Rakow took me on these fully punishing marathon runs out at Wilderness, any time I bitched and moaned too much about wanting to kick Mike's ass for not being around. I think it was good for Rakow too, to get it out in the open. He's been pissed off at Mike for a lot of years for taking off and leaving me and Mom, even though she never told him about me. He was pissed at Mom too, I think, for not telling, but in a different way. I don't know. The whole situation made him mad. Anyway, we spent plenty of energy exhausting any stupid get-even plots we might have concocted." He rolled his eyes at the memory.

Two years ago, after we'd learned about the events surrounding our births, we discovered that Mr. Rakow had played a more active role in David's history than we'd known. And that he had in fact, been friends with David's father. After these revelations, David and Mr. Rakow had gone through a few weeks of huffy coldness before Jen and I finally threatened to lock them in a room together unless they figured their shit out.

Of course, they'd gone out to Wilderness Park. That's where most of our emotionally charged conversations happened. Even though Jen and I weren't along on that first trip, I could see it happening in my mind's eye.

There would be no talking in the car on the way there. The dogs would be in the back seat of Rakow's car, each with their own open window. David would be staring stonily out the passenger side.

It would take the first half mile or so of walking just to get to the point where they could start talking. And then one of them would start. Probably David. They would walk side by side, and talk on the cleared path, occasionally chucking sticks for the dogs to chase or detouring off the path whenever the dogs wanted to investigate the creek.

They'd be walking side by side, never looking directly at each other. Somehow that, plus the privacy of the trees and the distraction of the dogs was enough to make the talking come easier. Or maybe that was magic, too. An everyday, earthy kind of magic. If things got too heavy, they might run for a bit. Tati was the best at sensing when that was needed, and would position herself on the path in front of them, running ahead and then looking back over her shoulder, inviting them to join her.

When they came back, there was a renewed easiness between them. David didn't tell us everything afterwards, but he did say Rakow thought Mike had a good heart. He also said he had a habit of getting super wound up in other people's problems and making questionable decisions. I wondered if maybe that's how he and Donna had connected in the first place.

Rakow liked Mike, but hated that he was fickle and flighty. By the time Donna knew she was pregnant with David, Mike had moved on from her little problems and gotten himself all hung up with a bunch of dope smoking pseudo-intellectuals who wanted to change the world. When Mike ran off to California with the rest of the peace-and-love hippies to dodge the draft and free his mind, he left behind not only Donna and a percolating David, but also Rakow, who had to step up in his place, both as a soldier, and as a friend.

I don't know if Rakow was always as *Sargeant* Rakow as he was now, but I bet he was a pretty practical, responsible teenager. I could certainly see how Mike leaving would piss him off. I could also see how it tore at David, knowing that his biological dad had bailed out, but still feeling the need to protect at least the idea of Mike as a good guy. Like, he had to be a good guy, right? Because he was part of David, and David was totally a good guy.

Over the course of the last couple of years, I'd sensed a deepening of the relationship between Mr. Rakow and David. It felt like now that all that history was out in the open between them, they knew where they stood. They were solid. Even so, I knew, and Jen and Jon knew, that David still held fast to the precious, treasured idea that his dad was somebody special. A dreamer maybe, a crappy dad maybe, but somebody really great.

"So," I mused. "You don't want to punch him until he's sorry. But, do you want to talk to him?"

David meditatively chewed the last fry. "I don't know," he said finally. "But I do want to meet him. Then, I think, I'll decide if I want to talk to him or not. Does that make any sense?"

"Totally," Jen nodded decisively. "First, we take his measure. Then, we decide if an ass-kicking is warranted. If not, then perhaps conversation."

Elaborate fist bumping followed and we pointed Clint for home. I hoped Jon's burger and the dogs' chicken tenders would still be warm by the time we got there, but I knew we weren't quite done talking yet. A few blocks from home, I sighed, and said the thing that had been bugging me uncomfortably since we left campus.

"I don't want to lay any jinxes on this, David, but I gotta ask. What if he's just awful?" I gave him a concerned look.

"Yeah, man," Jen said sadly. "Like, I really hope he's not, but he could be a complete jerk, or even worse, *evil*." She said it like it was a joke, but with our history, it kinda was and kinda wasn't. Ugh.

"Same here," David said, nodding. Relief that this possibility had already occurred to him flooded through me. "From what I've been able to get out of Rakow and Lorraine, he isn't *evil*, or he wasn't back then, anyway. In fact, I think Lorraine might have had a crush on him in high school. She made some moony comment about how *charismatic* he was back then."

He waggled his fingers and winked at Jen who raised one eyebrow. Blue words blossomed in my notebook with only a couple errors: *Evil? Probly not. Jerk? Don't no. Charisma – hinky? Watch and see.*

We pulled up to the house, and before David could open the passenger door, I grabbed his arm and he turned to face me. I put my hand to his forehead and took in a deep, physical and magical breath. I smelled the strong, sunshiny aroma of blooming lavender.

"Mom topped you off with some off her patented *Vitamin L*, you remember how that plays out, right? She's boosted us before," I said to him.

"Yeah! I'll be on top of my game until about," he flipped my wrist over to look at my watch. "Eleven tonight, when I'll sleep like a happy baby for eight solid hours and wake up feeling refreshed and alive. I freaking love your mom's *Vitamin L*," he grinned and high fived me. "I'm good to go!"

As if to prove it, he gathered up all the fast-food debris along with Jon's burger and the dogs' chicken and jumped out of the car. Tati and Shadow were already there and waiting, tongues lolling.

"Jen?" I asked. "Any portents, visions or hinky intuitions to share?"

Jen grasped Clint's steering wheel for a second, then relaxed – deliberately. She said, "Yeah, maybe, but I don't know what to make of it. A pink triangle. And it turns," she traced the shape in the air. "From point down, to point up. I've dreamed it the last three nights and the image has been in my head all day."

"*Cerebrum Scribe*" I whispered, retrieving the notebook I'd just shoved in my pocket. "Spinning pink triangle?" I asked, watching happily as the words magically appeared, correctly spelled for once, on the page. "It's not ringing any bells. I'll check it out."

Jen nodded. "To the library with you, Nancy Drew!"

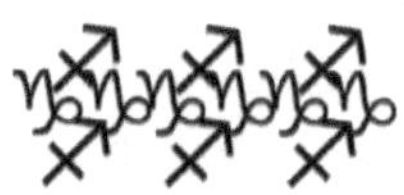

THE MYSTERY OF the pink triangle lasted exactly thirty seconds beyond my getting to the library and asking Nicole what the symbol might represent.

She looked at me wide-eyed and shook her head a little. "How could you, how could we have missed this?" She shook her head in exasperation.

I almost protested, before I recognized it as a hypothetical question and kept my mouth shut and my eyes and ears open. Nicole glanced around the library, which was empty at the moment except for an older guy reading a newspaper by the north window.

"Go snag your usual table," she said to me. "I'll be

right there." Something was clearly afoot. I did as I was bidden.

My favorite table was in the quietest back corner of adult nonfiction. It was clearly visible from the library's big front desk but also somewhat separate from the rest of the seating areas. I plunked my heavy backpack down on the table and dug out my notebook and pen.

Nicole returned with two books in one hand and a newspaper tucked under her arm. She put the books face-down on the table and kept the newspaper where it was. I automatically reached for the books, but she gently swatted my hand away.

"Listen first," she said quietly, leaning against the table. Her outfit today consisted of a long black skirt and a many-layered, purple, gauzy top with tiny round mirrors embellishing the embroidered mandala patterns. As usual she smelled of something exotic and spicy.

"The pink triangle has a gruesome and tragic history, but that's not all it has. But we must begin at the beginning." She patted the books on the table.

My heart sank. Even though I hadn't seen the titles yet, I'd seen the call numbers. 940.531. Nazis. Crap. Anything that began with Nazis couldn't be good.

"I know you pretty well, Angie," Nicole said, frankly. I know you've seen enough awful things to make you realize that humans can be the worst monsters of all."

I nodded and frowned. She was right. I knew lots about rotten, messed up humans doing terrible things. Like Charlie Starkweather and Caril going on their killing spree, like the Pale Man and his friend Chachi running their child trafficking ring, like Miss Jeanne, Nicole's predecessor here at the library who I held ultimately responsible for David's mom's death. People could be and were horrible with disturbing frequency.

And then, there were Nazis.

"You've probably seen pictures of Jewish holocaust survivors with the yellow Star of David on their sleeves, right? Nicole asked.

"Right," I confirmed.

"Did you know those stars were the symbol worn by only one of the groups the Nazis imprisoned in their concentration camps?" she asked.

"I know there were other people put in the camps, like people with mental illnesses and drug addicts," I said. "Oh, and Gypsies, right? Didn't Pat say something about the Roma being targeted in World War II?"

"Yes. Those people wore a black triangle, point down," Nicole nodded. "Along with vagrants, pacificists, prostitutes and lesbians."

*Crap.*

"Emigrants got a blue triangle. Political prisoners like socialists, Freemasons, and Gentiles who assisted Jews wore red." She paused.

"Who wore pink?" I asked.

"Homosexual men," she replied. "These two books are memoirs from that time." She turned them gently over and showed me the covers of the books she held, one by Heinz Heger, the other by Richard Plant. The pink triangle, point down, was prominently displayed on both. "I won't keep them from you, of course, but I would highly recommend waiting and reading these a year or two from now. Maybe in a college class where you'll have far more context and a professor on hand to answer any questions, but ultimately that's up to you and your folks."

I gave both books a careful once over, noted the author's names in my notebook, and then set them aside and looked at Nicole.

"You said this isn't everything?" I asked.

"That's right." Nicole lifted a gauzy layer from her top and exposed a round pin affixed to the underlayer, out of sight but near her heart. On a black background, the pink triangle stood out brightly, point up. Underneath, in all caps in white it read SILENCE = DEATH.

Nicole's eyes were bright with energy and emotion. "A couple of years ago, in New York City, an activist named Larry Kramer gave a speech that inspired a lot of people to do something about the way the government was ignoring the AIDS epidemic. That included this group, ACT UP. They chose the pink triangle, point up, as their logo and their rallying cry. They took the symbol away from its Nazi beginnings, and remade it as something positive and hopeful. They stage really dramatic protests, like hundreds of people lying down and playing dead to block traffic on Wall Street."

I sighed; my heart heavy. AIDS had been all over the news pretty much since I could remember. AIDS was culturally unlike other viruses that wreaked havoc like the 1918 flu, or Polio in the whole first half of the 20th century. Because those diseases had targeted mainly young people and little kids, there was a huge outcry to find cures. But since AIDS seemed to target mainly gay men, public opinion was loaded with fear, bigotry, and misconceptions. Lots of people went so far as to think the AIDS virus was some sort of righteous hand-of-God thing sent to kill sinners.

Of course, if you knew even the first thing about science, you'd know that viruses don't play by the same rules as human ethicists. Viruses are on a singular mission to survive and they'll use whatever means necessary to achieve it. To viruses, humans are simply handy vessels they can use to reproduce. But that didn't stop people at the time from blaming or ignoring victims, dragging their feet on medical research, or just being generally awful about the whole thing.

Nicole took the newspaper from under her arm and lay it down. "This isn't a library copy, it's mine. I just wanted to show you the publisher's name."

I unfolded the paper and looked at the front page. It was titled "The Body Politic, A Gay Liberation Newspaper." Nicole opened it and pointed to the publisher's information. "Pink Triangle Press." The paper was dated December of last year. I glanced over the articles briefly, and one caught my eye. It was a story about a protest held on November 27th, the anniversary of the death of someone named Harvey Milk. At the end there was a list of names of the twenty-three protesters who'd been arrested at the event. Included in those names were the three organizers: Elizabeth Darby, Jim Segal, and Mike Ellis.

Crap. If Mike was connected to the symbol Jen was seeing, then suddenly I had a whole lot of research to do about Mike.

A little help would be nice.

That thought had barely crossed my mind when the front door of the library whooshed open. Nicole turned on her librarian face to greet the newcomer, and then smiled more naturally when she saw Jen walk in. Jen walked directly over and sat down next to me.

"So, we have some sleuthing to do?" She asked, digging a pen from her backpack.

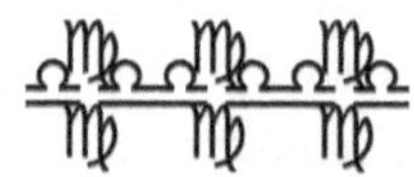

IT TOOK US several days, a trip to the downtown library and at least two dozen calls to Nicole and Lisa's librarian friend and their contacts to exhaust our avenues of inquiry about Mike, but we found out quite a bit.

Much of what we discovered came in the way of publicly accessible arrest records. In fact, those helped us trace Mike's path over the last 19 years, from Nebraska to Los Angeles, through a period of frequent crisscrossing the country with regular stops in places like Austin, Madison, and Chicago, then he stayed mostly quiet for a while up around Oregon, and for the last couple of years, back in L.A. He'd had quite the adventurous life.

When we'd started recreating Mike's path using police records, Jen had snagged a big US map that came with her mom's car insurance and started using it as a magical focus. With her guidance, we were able to pinpoint towns where she sensed he'd been, then contact the librarians in that town for local information.

That's when we discovered that many of his youthful indiscretions had happened during his time on the road working for the band, Lucid Absurdity. Once we had that piece of the puzzle, Nicole started searching art and music 'zines from that time period, of which there were many. The band got a few mentions in *Creem* and *Bomp*, but then she hit the motherload. She stumbled onto a 'zine called *Sojourner* that was more or less obsessed with Lucid Absurdity until they broke up in 1974. This one writer apparently followed them to every rehearsal, gig, demo recording and raucous after-party for the better part of two years.

On Saturday the 25th, we reconvened at the library to pull together everything we'd learned about Mike, and to decide what, if anything, to do with what we'd learned.

Nicole perched at the edge of our study table where

she could keep an eye on the circulation desk and the front door. Sitting beside her was a stack of *Sojourners* on loan to us from the private collection of a record store owner she knew. Judging from their musty smell, his private collection must have been housed in his basement, but the pages were intact, if faded and worn.

In those pages we read about the lead singer, Jim Segal's "mind expanding lyrics" and the lead guitar player's "freaky chill riffs" as well as their penchant for "exotic days-long party jags." Reviews of nearly every performance were capped off with "The police were called in at 2:50 a.m." or "Jim and three others were arrested for disturbing the peace," or "The party raged until 4:00 a.m. when the ambulance arrived. Two people were hospitalized with overdoses." Mike's name was mentioned in some of the stories, most often as the person who bailed the others out of jail or rescheduled the next show, but also occasionally being transported to a hospital or a local constabulary, as my dad would say.

"Guys, listen to this." She held up the one dated December of 1974 and read aloud. "The thrill is gone. Lucid Absurdity has lost Jim Segal, the heart and soul of the band. The band's final performance with Segal at the microphone officially happened last night at the English Disco on the Sunset Strip, but it could be argued that the end had been coming for months. Ever since last summer, when rumors swirled that at the heart of Jim's breakup with his long-time girlfriend Pam was her secret love affair with Jim's good friend and road manager, Mike Ellis, the band has been struggling to regain their creative footing. Their new album, slated for a January release, is permanently shelved."

"Ooo," I said. "A juicy love triangle." I looked at our timeline. "December of 1974, that's close to when Mike goes north to Oregon for a while. Does it say anything about what happened to Pam? Did she and Mike run away together?"

Jen slowly and deliberately traced one long fingernail down a stack of photocopied newspaper articles. Near the bottom, she stopped and carefully pinched one out of the pile. "Doesn't look that way."

She read to us from a photocopy of an obituary from the San Francisco Chronicle, dated January 1975. "'Pamela Winnefred Baxter, artist, adventurer and beloved daughter, 11/21/53-1/12/75 passed from this earth far too soon. Survived by her parents Jane and Philip Baxter,' etcetera etcetera. It doesn't say how she died."

"Just that she died young. Well that stinks," I said. "Then we have a little evidence of Mike in Oregon for the next couple years, he's mentioned here," I pointed to a paper-clipped stack of copied news articles from the *Tillamook Headlight* as a co-founder of an after-school program for troubled kids in 1977, "and then here again in 1980 organizing a rally for Jimmy Carter's reelection campaign, before he lost to Reagan."

"Was that the first mention of him doing anything political?" Nicole asked, flipping through another stack of photocopies neatly labeled "1980-82" and frowning.

"I believe so, and that doesn't really ramp up until here," I handed them an article about the New York City Lesbian and Gay Pride March in 1983, dedicated to the victims of AIDS. "Here he's listed as an organizer for a group who drove from California to New York for this protest. There are a couple arrest records from protests from '83 to '86, but nothing major. Trespassing, disturbing the peace, that sort of stuff.

"But then we get a new rash of them here," I pointed to my timeline, "starting in the spring of 1987. It looks like whatever group he was protesting with started to get really radical around that time. He was arrested three times that summer, and then last year, another four times. Two protests that got out of hand and did some property damage, one looks like a fight, and this one says, misdemeanor drug possession." I frowned. "That's the first mention of drugs since he moved to Oregon. I was kind of hoping that was when he got his act together. I wonder what happened to get things riled up again?"

Jen's eyes unfocused just slightly and my necklace warmed against my collarbone. She blinked and then turned to Nicole.

"What is the date on the most recent of those *Sojourner* 'zines?" she asked.

"I think they quit publishing in about '78," she mused, flipping through the stack and pulling a copy from the bottom. "Wait!" She'd held up the February, 1978 issue and two carefully torn out pages slipped out onto the table. "What's this?"

Stuck into the fold of the final edition were two color magazine articles from two years ago, both by the same journalist who'd written most of the articles about the band, Lucid Absurdity. A guy by the name of Dominic Bruni. One was from a magazine called *The Face*; the other was *Roling Stone*.

The *Rolling Stone* article was brief. It mentioned Jim Segal had performed two songs at a Gay and Lesbian Pride gathering the night before a march. The article in *The Face* was longer, and it had pictures.

Nicole read part of it aloud. "Jim Segal, sole surviving member of Lucid Absurdity, is back on the music scene, this time for a great cause. He's lending his star power and still-potent musical talents to a political organization called, Act Up! Los Angeles and is working to bring attention to victims of the AIDS crisis.

"This reporter got the chance to interview him after his recent gig at the Pasadena Playhouse. When asked what inspired him to get back into music, he responded simply, 'AIDS. I was diagnosed with the AIDS virus six months ago. I was fortunate to receive some great support and help from an old friend and from friends in the Gay and Lesbian community. These people have been fighting to bring light and help to the victims battling this deadly disease tirelessly for years now. But we're running out of time. If the President doesn't make sure that the medical community has the resources they need to do this work and find some real help for people like me soon, it'll be too late. I may only have a couple more years to live. If I can help, if I can bring more attention to the problem, maybe something will get done.'

"'What do you want to tell our readers, Jim?' 'I want to tell them to educate themselves. Talk to people in your community and find out what's really happening. Even though this disease has hit the gay and lesbian community hard, that's not the whole story. I'm not gay, but I did have an addiction problem. When I got clean from heroin, I thought I had my whole life ahead of me. But AIDS can be transferred from shared needles, and from unprotected hetero sex. I don't even know for sure how I got it, but now I'm fighting for my life. I want to tell them to call their representatives in Washington. Tell them Americans are dying needlessly. There are medicines out there that can help us, but we need to be able to access them. We can't be afraid to meet this head on. Silence only equals death!'"

There was a half-page, color picture with the article, a wide shot of the stage from the audience's point of view. Jim was front and center, singing. He was thin. Very thin. His cheeks were hollow and there were circles under his eyes. The guitar player and drummer with him looked vibrantly healthy by comparison. Behind him and to the left, just off stage, a couple people were watching. One of them caught my eye. His dark hair and eyes looked familiar.

"Is that Mike?" I asked pointing.

Jen peered at it closely. "I think, yes."

"Looks like they've gotten the band back together," quipped Nicole.

"It makes me think about what Mr. Rakow said," I mused aloud, "that Mike was forever getting mixed up in other people's drama. It seems like he's right. Mike's heart is in the right place, but he can't seem to stay away from drama."

"Right," Jen said, stacking her notes carefully. "And other people's drama is pretty unpredictable. So, we stay alert and watch David's back." She scooted her chair back and started to get up, then paused, rubbing her temple. We waited, breathlessly while she processed the vision she was seeing.

Jen looked at me, tilted her head like she was trying to make sense of something and said, "Tell your mom. Tell your mom to watch out for drama." She shook her head a little and shrugged. We both knew better than to question it.

"I'm on it," I responded.

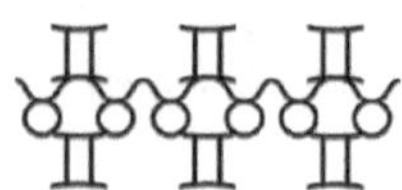

IT HAD BEEN decided that David's dad, Mike, would

come over to Lorraine's at eight o'clock on Sunday night, the 26th. Everyone was scheduled to go to work and school the next day, which gave us a limited timeframe. That way if things went somehow off the rails or just got way too emotionally intense, we had a built-in excuse to wrap it up and send everybody home.

*Everyone* was us kids, Lorraine, Rakow, and my folks. It was cold and blustery out, so Lorraine sent us out to the garage early to fire up the space heaters and arrange tables and chairs. With the heaters going, the garage became a cozy den, redolent with the aromas of sage and cloves, and a hint of fabric softener.

At precisely 7:59 p.m. a white Chevy Astro van pulled up in front of Lorraine's driveway.

My folks were already in the garage, seated at a card table, my mom warming her perpetually cold hands and feet at one of the heaters. Jen, Jon, David and I were milling around the table where Lorraine had us set up cups, a pitcher of water and a thermos of decaf, along with four boxes of Girl Scout cookies she'd bought from the neighbor kid. Lorraine bustled over with napkins in one hand and tissue boxes under her arm.

"Are two boxes of tissues enough?" She asked, setting down her things.

"I'm more concerned whether four boxes of Girl Scout cookies will be enough," I said to her, watching the boys decimate a whole sleeve of Thin Mints.

Lorraine and Rakow went outside to greet Mike. The driver of the van beeped the horn and took off. The three of approached the garage, chatting.

I examined their faces closely as they stepped inside. Lorraine entered first, smiling broadly in what seemed to me intense optimism tinged by nervousness. Mike came through the door next, followed by a sour faced Mr.

Rakow.

My eyes widened. I heard Jen's low murmur, "Oh, my!"

Mike was far and away the most amazingly handsome guy either one of us had ever seen in person. Don't get me wrong, David was good looking in the extreme. His dark hair and eyes coupled with that playful grin plus the extreme workout schedule he maintained with Rakow combined to guarantee he had zero problems attracting admirers. But Mike was, like, *wow*.

Mike was off the charts, movie star, male model, god-who-fell-to-earth good looking. He wasn't just handsome. He was *beautiful*. His hair was long and dark, wavy down his back and curling at the ends. It was tucked behind his ears, and only a little flattened by the hat he removed when he came inside. He had a closely trimmed beard and mustache that framed a smiling mouth. His skin was suntanned brown and glowing with good health. His eyes were just a slightly darker shade of amber than David's.

Jen very deliberately set down her water glass, picked up a napkin and delicately wiped her mouth, never once taking her eyes off him. I held my breath so I wouldn't give in to the helpless and completely inappropriate giggles clamoring to be let out.

Mike wore faded blue jeans, worn desert boots, and a colorful woven pullover. He smelled like sandalwood and burning grass. In one hand, he carried his brown felt hat. I glimpsed a tiny silver key peeking out of the hat band.

My folks stood to greet him. "Are you *watching*?" I whispered to Jon. His ability to *see* the essence of a thing or a person might provide us with useful clues.

"I am," he whispered back, his face alight.

"Something interesting?" I murmured in his ear.

"I could write a book on this! It's — wow!"

I raised my eyebrows in reply and refocused my own attention on the scene transpiring.

"Mike," my dad said. "I'm Alden Parsons. David has been a friend of our family for many years, but particularly so since Donna's car accident a few years back. I'm very pleased to make your acquaintance. Please meet my wife, and Angie's mother, Elizabeth." He nodded my way and then motioned my mom to step closer.

The brief glance Mike directed my way at my dad's introduction nearly made my heart stop.

"Steady, love." Jon whispered, "There's something — curious going on here."

*Hmm. Curious, but not hinky, what might that mean? And why was I feeling lightheaded? Oh yeah, breathe.*

"Mr. Parsons, Mrs. Parsons, I'm so glad to meet you! Please accept my gratitude for taking David and Donna into your family along with Lorraine and Rakow here." He gestured towards the door were a very growly looking Rakow lurked. Hands were shaken all around.

Then he turned our way. "Lorraine told me she and Jack had twins, and you two look quite a lot like your parents! Hi Jen, Hi Jon. Nice to meet you both."

He shook hands genially when he introduced himself to my folks, but he looked a bit bewildered about how to address us kids. We did nothing to ease his discomfiture, preferring to watch and see how he dealt with uncertainty. He fiddled with his fingers for a second and then shook it off and turned to me with a big smile.

"Hi Angie, it's nice to meet you as well." I nodded, trying to keep my face neutral. It was hard, because everything about Mike really wanted you to like him. He practically radiated positivity and hope.

David took a step forward to stand face to face with

his dad. They stood silently like that for a moment, taking one another in. Same dark, shiny brown hair, David's a little shaggy, Mike's long hair hung past his shoulder blades. Same amber-brown eyes. Same lean, muscular build, and nearly the same height. Mike's mustache and neatly trimmed goatee would look pretty great on David too, once he had enough whiskers to manage it.

Mike reached out and clasped David's shoulders. That's when I felt both Jon and my mom perk up. I watched closely. I felt the faint warmth of my living stone necklace at my collarbone.

"David," Mike said thoughtfully. "She chose the name David for you; did she ever say why?"

David shook his head, eyes locked on his father's. I expected him to be tense, or at least a little nervous, but he seemed neither. On the contrary, he seemed completely open to whatever this man was laying down.

"David was my grandad's name," Mike went on. "He adored your mom. Always asked me to bring her around the nursing home whenever we spoke. Donna thought the sun rose and set on him. He was a good, and a kind man. Everyone loved him. She couldn't have chosen a better name."

David smiled like he did when he heard a particularly satisfactory guitar riff for the first time.

Mike continued to look closely at David, like he was inspecting him from the inside out. "Things were hard for you," Mike said quietly, his gaze softening. "She was…"

Something was passing between the two of them. I glanced, frowning at Jon and then my mom. Jon was nearly as entranced as David, but Mom, although she was monitoring the scene closely, caught my eye and gave me an *It's okay* sort of look. I surreptitiously opened my notebook and whispered, *Cerebrum Scribe*. Notes began appearing on the blank page in blue ink.

Mike looked like he'd entered some sort of trance. His amber eyes, so like David's, zigged back and forth like he was reading, or watching something on fast forward. Fleeting expressions crossed his face, first laughter, then sadness, and fear. I saw him flinch a few times, and once his arm jerked hard and from where I stood, I could see redness bloom on the back of one hand. A circular red spot — like a cigarette burn. His eye, his left one, the same eye David lost when Mitch hit him with the broken gear shifter, twitched and went totally dark.

Mike's fingers tightened on David's shoulders and tears flowed freely from his eyes.

"My dear boy, you've endured so much," he murmured in a low, compassionate voice. "How did you…"

That's when I saw David's necklace really light up. Even without the visible beams of colored light that sometimes connected our necklaces, I felt the palpable sense of our bond. My heart pounded. My face flushed. The feeling I got after the three of us had kicked some particularly scary monster butt, like that Troll, or the Eridani flowed over me. Strong. Proud. Victorious.

Mike's face lit up like fireworks at the Fourth of July.

"By the sun and stars boy, look at you! You have the strength of giants and the heart of a warrior! How…Rakow?" Mike turned, confused and awed, to look at Rakow and Lorraine.

Just then there was a ruckus at the door. Tati and Shadow, who most likely had been dozing downstairs on David's bed, chose this moment to make their appearance. Mr. Rakow, who had been standing by the door this whole time looking like he'd swallowed a bug, reached over and flicked the door open to let them in.

Both dogs went from sleepyhead mode to extremely

interested mode in the time it took for them to trot across the garage to where David and Mike were standing. David placed his own hands gently atop Mike's which still rested on his shoulders and with a gentle squeeze, removed them.

"Mike, this is Shadow and Tati," David indicated each dog as he spoke. Mike gave him, and then Rakow, another surprised glance before addressing the dogs.

Jon leaned in over my shoulder. "Watch the dogs," he whispered in my ear.

Mike reached out one hand each to the dogs. I watched breathlessly.

While Tati gave Mike's shoes a careful going-over, Shadow sniffed Mike's right hand deeply. This was no cursory sniff. Shadow was *seriously* interested. Mike smiled.

Mike's smile was something else. When David smiled, there was often an impish light behind his eyes. David was forever looking for a laugh, or a challenge. His smile was an invitation to adventure. Mike's smile was like the sun coming out from behind a cloud, or a baby's laugh. You felt yourself immediately smiling back, and feeling this bone-deep gladness.

Shadow promptly sat. He had turned nine this year, and although he was hale and hearty, it was becoming clearer, particularly since last year's run-in with the Eridani, that Shadow was slowing down. He napped more, got up and down more slowly, and was quickly earning the title of King of the long-suffering dog sigh.

Sitting there looking up at Mike, he offered up a paw which Mike respectfully shook, then ruffled Shadow's ears with his other hand.

"Watch!" Jon whispered excitedly.

To my eyes, the change was subtle. When both Mike's hands touched Shadow's fur, Shadow's eyes brightened. His jaw dropped and his tongue lolled happily. When Mike released Shadow, he bounded to his feet, did a little spin, licked David's hand then trotted over to Mr. Rakow. Shadow gave a playful little hop then bumped his head under Rakow's hand for a good rub, which was, of course, granted. There was a noticeable uptick in the older dog's energy.

Then, Tati leaped daintily up into David's arms. That was part of a thing they did during their regular workouts. I'm pretty sure the inspiration for it had a lot to do with Luke and Yoda's training on Dagobah. He'd trained Tati to ride on his back in a kind of backpack/sling he and Rakow had cobbled together while he ran. She did so happily when he asked, although typically she preferred to run alongside.

She leaped up gracefully, and he caught her with the ease of long practice. She gave him a quick snuffle and kiss to the chest before turning her attention on Mike.

I watched, enthralled. The dogs had often alerted us to hinkiness of the paranormal persuasion, but even more importantly, they were both really excellent judges of human character. Mike had already passed Shadow's test with flying colors, and had apparently gotten juiced with some kind of good mojo in the process. I held my breath and watched to see what Tati would make of him.

She twisted around in David's arms so she was facing Mike. He smiled that megawatt smile at her and she reached out and very deliberately and delicately placed a paw on Mike's forehead – directly between his eyebrows. Mike held very still.

I frowned, puzzled. Typically, if Tati touched us with her paws, she touched our hands. Only our hands. She was kind of particular about it, in fact. Shadow didn't use paw touches at all. If he wanted your attention, he used his big head or some version of a body block. He wasn't the subtlest of dogs.

Tati was daintier in her communication. She used the, sit-pretty-and-bore-my-bright-eyes-directly-into-the-human technique, which usually meant something obvious like, *Lurking interdimensional beastie in yonder hedge!* or, *The water dish is empty!*

She had the best *Let's-go-play!* fanny wiggle in the world, and she had the hand touch. For David, there was also the thing where she laid her head against his chest and reached up and touched his throat with her nose, which was both freaking adorable, and reserved solely for David.

This forehead touch was new. Totally unique. The gentleness of the motion and the specific delicacy of placement had me super curious.

Then for a few seconds, everything and everyone in the garage seemed overlaid with a deep indigo light, and just as suddenly it was gone. Tati gave Mike a pleased little lick on the nose, hopped down from David's arms, and trotted off to investigate whatever Shadow was now sniffing at under the crack of the garage door.

"What was that?" I asked Jon under my breath. Nobody else said word one about it, although from the looks on their faces, I was sure at least Lorraine and my mom had both seen it too. They just blabbed the sorts of happy, polite things you say when your dog likes someone new. At least that's what Lorraine and my dad did. Rakow just kept low key-glowering.

"I think that's what mom would call his aura. It's similar to the life essence that I *see* when I look at him, but different, too," Jon whispered back. "You'll have to ask mom for details, but I think Mike's either a Jedi, or more likely, an *Inorog*, and a really strong one, at that." He was perched against the edge of one of the sturdier tables, leaning forward so his chin rested on my shoulder, his voice low in my ear.

"Jedi?" I whispered, grinning. "You wish."

I'd seen references to Inorogs in the Coven's library.

*You heard me right, the Coven has a library. But that's a whole other story. Maybe I'll tell you that one sometime.*

Inorogs were people supposedly touched by unicorns and gifted with a big magical dose of intuition and empathy that they could tap into. Or maybe it tapped into them. I wasn't clear on what the real story was, but there was clearly something to it, if Mike was any proof. ***Research Inorogs*** appeared in bold blue ink in my notebook, and the page flipped itself with a little shiver of geeky excitement.

"She touched his head chakra, didn't she?" I whispered to Jen who leaned against the table on my other side.

"Bingo," Jen whispered back. "Mom's been wondering if that has anything to do with the way David has been communicating with the dogs. You know how she always touches David's chest? Then she started touching his throat, his fifth chakra, and when that started happening, David and Tati were in tune on a whole other level."

"The throat chakra is about communication, right?"

"Right. And the one in the forehead, the sixth chakra, the one she touched on Mike, that's the imagination and intuition chakra."

My dad and Lorraine took turns sort of leading the conversation after that, getting Mike caught up on the last eighteen or so years of David's history, strategically glossing over our supernatural extracurriculars for another conversation on another day, maybe. Whenever the talk bordered on our work, Lorraine or Dad would redirect and ask what had been happening for Mike.

He was open about his past, which seemed like a good sign.

"I toured with Jim and his band for a couple of years, and it was phenomenal," Mike said. He was sitting with the rest of us, scattered here and there in folding chairs around a couple of folding tables pushed together. The water, cookies and tissues had already been passed around and made good use of.

"Jim is such an amazingly talented musician," he went on, "but he was real troubled, back then. We were all partying way too much, of course. It went with the territory. It took me years afterwards to quit drinking, it nearly did me in. But Jim was into harder stuff, too. Coke and heroin. It messed him up real bad." He sighed, took a swig of decaf and patted his pocket, then pulled his hand away and took a deep breath, evidently reminding himself that Lorraine didn't allow cigarette smoking in the garage

"I don't want to subject you guys to a bunch of gory details, but the long and short of it is, Jim's girlfriend Pam cheated on him with me, and that ended everything. Pam left. She should have gone home to her parents, they were strict, but they might have been able to keep her alive." He started to reach for his pocket again, and changed direction mid-reach to his coffee. He swirled it around, but didn't drink. "I don't know, maybe nothing could have. She was a wonderful and complicated person. And she died. Badly."

"When Jim found out about Pam, he just fell apart. The band fell apart. Everything. He was living on the streets, broke and completely messed up on drugs. I got out of L.A. and got my shit together, as well as I could anyway. It took a while.

"I made some friends. I found a good rehab that

would take me. After I got straight, I started helping out in whatever ways I could. The rehab center I'd gone to was seeing kids come in that weren't even in their teens yet. It was a crazy time. I worked with them for quite a while."

Mike mostly looked at his hands while he was telling this story, so he missed it, but I didn't. Mr. Rakow's shoulders relaxed just a tiny bit at this point. His frown eased slightly and he looked more like his usual stoic self, less like his crabby irritable self.

"And then, one of the kids I was trying to help got sick. By the time he got to see a doctor, AIDS had already destroyed his immune system. He was 15 when he died." He paused to accept the tissue box my mom had pushed his way. "Thanks, Mrs. Parsons. I won't lie, it hit me hard. Once I got done being pissed off about it, I started trying to learn more about it. That got me involved with lots of groups of activists who were working to change the laws that are in the way of getting people the help they need.

"I was back in LA, organizing a protest when I ran into Jim. He'd just gotten his AIDS diagnosis a month or two before, and was still reeling. Some mutual friends brought us back together." He took a slug of coffee and his face brightened. "We talked all night. My best friend was back." Mike sniffed and scrubbed at his face with a tissue unselfconsciously.

"I don't know what to say about Jim that will give you a real sense of him. I hope you'll be able to meet him and see for yourself. He's done so much in such a short time, and he's had a mountain of battles to fight the whole way. He's given so much of himself, his talent, his precious energy to this movement. With his words and his music, he's brought literally thousands of people into the organization and reached countless thousands more."

Mike paused and looked at David, like he was willing him to understand. "And his precious energy is in short supply. This trip to DC will probably be his last performance. He doesn't have much time left. He was adamant that we stop here, though, on the way. He always loved to hear me talk about Lincoln. I guess I made it sound pretty good to him. And then when Lorraine's letter found us, he insisted. So, he arranged for the group of folks, people he himself has recruited, to meet up here in town. We'll all leave together in a few days for the east coast. But this has given him a few days respite from travelling, and I'm grateful for it. He's just so fragile these days –" he tapered off.

Intense sadness, regret, anger, respect and wonder all filled me in a more intimate, more vibrant way than I was accustomed to. This just wasn't my normal emotional intensity level. My hinky radar was beeping quietly. I swallowed my brain's very demanding desire to ugly cry. Then I noticed the fading aura of blue all around us.

Wow, wow! Mike's feelings had become not only visible, but we had like, absorbed them! And if they hadn't caused us to intensely feel those same emotions, at the least they had amped up our experience of them. And I was like, a thousand percent sure he wasn't doing it deliberately. I was a little wigged out and a lot curious. My notebook's pages flipped so quickly it looked like they were in a stiff breeze.

*Crap*

Mike drained his coffee and looked around sheepishly.

"I'm sorry," he said in a low tone. "This has just been a pretty crazy time, especially the last couple months. And then," he looked up and smiled at Lorraine who smiled back, her eyes bright with tears. "I lucked onto Lorraine's letter and this whole new story has fallen open to me, I'm a bit overwhelmed." Then he looked around like he was once again just noticing his surroundings. "It must be late, we've been talking so long, I should let you kind people be."

And then, a bunch of things happened all at once.

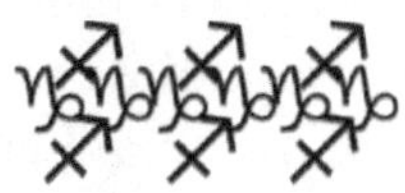

TATI AND SHADOW roused from their spots under the snack table and leapt into motion.

Shadow veered to sniff at the air around the garage door sill, a low rumble in his chest, which usually meant a car had pulled up outside the house. Then Tati bolted for the human-sized door and barked her very excited, friend-at-the-door bark.

Lorraine strode towards the door behind Tati and Rakow followed on her heels, his eyes still fixed on Shadow sniffing under the door.

A sudden sensation from my living stone necklace caught my attention. Unlike its usual glowing or humming, this felt like a sputter, or a shudder. Like Clint had done that time Jen and I blew off getting gas before school and Clint's tank ran dry when we left at lunch.

Then, Jen, who was to my right, stiffened. We all knew that meant a vision was about to kick in. In the space of about three seconds, I pushed my chair away behind me and dragged her, chair and all, a few more inches clear of the table into clear space while David snagged the big floor pillows off their low shelf and deftly tossed them at her feet. Jon positioned himself behind her in case she fell back, David and I drew close on either side.

Jen's ability to work with and around her visions had increased exponentially in the last years, but the full-body visions seemed intent on making sure she was paying close attention to the assignment, which typically meant big trouble was brewing. She stiffened and shook.

*Yikes and double yikes.*

The adults were all extra double focused on whatever was happening at the door and with the dogs.

"Speak, Prophet!" I hissed in her ear.

"War," she moaned. "War in the stars. Falling angels. Fire. Chaos! Slings and arrows. Tiny pinprick of light – too bright!" She covered her eyes and her voice cracked. "Brilliant…black…heartbreak." Tears were flowing down her cheeks and she was shaking.

Lorraine swung the door open wide. Outside stood a smiling, bone-thin man with the brightest eyes and a sweet smile that made you not want to notice the dreadful lesions on his face. But you did notice.

"Jim!" Mike sang out.

"I don't mean to interrupt, I'm so sorry, Mike. You said to come at ten and it's forty-five past. I just wanted to make sure you were doing okay?" The care and concern for Mike in his voice sounded a thousand percent genuine in my ears, but the look he was giving Mike felt more like, *We gotta go, now!*

"Please, come in, Jim," Lorraine encouraged.

Jim smiled and nodded gratefully at her and entered the room. He was about my height, with dark brown curly hair cut short. His eyes were a light shade of green set off nicely by his purple t-shirt. Pinned prominently to his jean jacket pocket was one of the Act Up pins, black with the bright pink triangle. The symbol that had set off our search in the first place. The symbol that Jen dreamed.

I turned to look at Jen and the boys, my eyes wide. Before I could utter a word, the dogs exploded into excited barking and Maka blew into the room on a blast of wintry wind looking every inch the shaman.

She also looked fully prepared to begin issuing orders and barely checked herself upon seeing strangers present. She gave Rakow and us a loaded look. David and I straightened up, extending our hands out to Jen where she sat. Jon had his hands on her shoulders while she caught her breath. She blinked, squeezed Jon's hand and waggled her fingers at us, before jumping up confidently. My folks were standing.

Mike took a look around at everyone, clapped his hands together and exclaimed, "Well my goodness! It looks as though it's time for us to say goodnight. David, can I call you tomorrow? I'd like to talk more, if you want?" He turned to David and gave him a hopeful smile.

Tati bounded over and rubbed her head against David's knee. Something was said. I am not privy to what. David smiled at her, then stuck out a hand and shook Mike's.

"Yeah, he said. "I think I'd like that."

Mike smiled hugely at David, quickly thanked Lorraine and joined his friend Jim who was already halfway down the driveway.

Lorraine watched them until they pulled away from the curb before turning to Maka. "Will we need the Coven?"

"We're going to need a miracle," replied Maka.

*Gulp.*

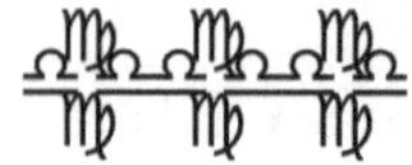

LORRAINE DASHED INSIDE to activate the Coven's emergency phone tree while Maka filled the rest of us in.

"Pilgrims are gathering in Lincoln. We've been tracking their movements since early evening. More and more are coming every hour. They're setting up stations on the cardinal points and their witches have been busy. They're doing a grid search of town – looking for the portal. It's only a matter of time before they discover it. Clara is there now with Alesta, Barb and Malinowski, going over all our protective spells, checking for holes and weak spots, but this is an organized attack. They WILL find the portal. And that's not the worst of it."

*Again, Gulp.*

"Near one of the spellmarkers Barb and Malinowski checked, they found an acid burn."

"More Eridani?" Rakow asked, keys in hand, ready to bolt for his arsenal as soon as Maka's briefing was done. The presence of Eridani would drastically alter the type of weapons we'd need.

"We have to prepare as if we are certain. We cannot afford false hope," she replied. "But there is one more thing," she cautioned before anyone could move. "The rate of the portal's decay is increasing. Within the boundaries of our protection spells, Earth's physics are being sorely tested. We're getting massive temperature and gravity fluctuations, at least one pocket of sulfuric acid, and several instances of seismic activity." Maka seemed as unflappable as ever, but my healing sense was telling me her heartrate was elevated.

All of our heartrates were elevated.

"We're going to want to suit up," Jen said.

"I'm bringing Barb and Malinowski their gear now. We'll meet you there," Maka said, striding toward the door. Rakow followed, Jen and David on his heels. I quickly kissed Jon, hugged my mom and followed.

Maka disappeared before I even got outside. Lorraine stood outside the kitchen door holding our go-bags. David grabbed his, gave Lorraine a quick peck on the cheek then said to us, "I'll go with Rakow to load up the weapons. You guys get there. See you in a flash." The three of us grasped hands and our necklaces lit up like Times Square. Then he was gone, running down the dark driveway to where Rakow's car idled at the curb.

Jen and I each planted a kiss on Lorraine's cheeks, and dashed off to climb into Clint, our heavy backpacks bumping against our legs. I dug into my mine. Jen pointed Clint towards the Wesleyan Campus and hit the gas. Clint obliged, seemingly making no concessions for the icy cold weather.

Lorraine took care of all the maintenance for the family cars, and as a result, all their vehicles not only ran smoothly with few if any mechanical issues, they got really kickass gas mileage and the tires were always full. Best of all during Nebraska winters, they started the first time every time, the windshields never fogged up and they never once had to scrape ice.

*Just like magic.*

Working with the Coven had many benefits, notably a radical improvement in our battle kits. From my backpack I pulled my winter-weight coverall. The summer one had a separate tactical vest, but the winter one was all one piece. Because it was designed by Rome, it also sported a gloriously wacky sort of 1950's era pink and green starburst pattern, the colors bewitched to blend in with your surroundings. The boys' version had 50's era planets and space ships and aircraft. It was both the craziest and best camouflage Rakow said he'd ever worn.

Since it was also designed by Deanne and my mom, it had healing spells woven into it. It wouldn't save you if you, say, had your head lopped off or spent over an hour in the vacuum of space, but for just about everything else, you stood a solid chance of survival. Because Lisa had a direct hand in its construction, it felt like you were wearing high performance cashmere.

Nicole, Elizabeth and Ginny had banded together to create a similar sort of armor the dogs could wear and were honestly about ready to give it up when Becky suggested tossing the armor idea wholesale and instead designing harnesses jam packed with spells. Specifically, spells that could be triggered either by the environment or remotely by Rakow or David. That worked like a charm. The dogs were now either equipped for or safe from: fire, flood, loss of oxygen, poisons – either liquid or gaseous, all knife and most bullet wounds, as well as poison ivy, ticks *and* fleas.

I checked and re-holstered knives from various locations, my forearm mounted arrow launcher, a line of tiny grenades on my left that launched spells, and slightly larger ones on my right that blew up enchanted shrapnel and adjusted my face mask. I didn't keep it on just yet, but when it was all on and locked in place, well, this suit was basically its own little armored universe, tailor made to protect me. Then I started checking Jen's equipment.

The witches had time, over the past two years, to manufacture at least two of these beauties for everybody. And after our throw-down with the Eridani last year, they were now also acid-proof and equipped with the magical

antidote to Eridani sucker toxin. We knew the toxin antidote worked, because we'd had to use it. We weren't able
to test the acid as much as we wanted, though. The samples we had left had degraded too quickly to be useful, so
Pat and Becky had done the best they could using earth
acids.

It was almost exactly a year ago that the three Eridani
had come through the portal and were dumped uncere-
moniously on the Wesleyan campus. We weren't sure
where in the galaxy they'd come from, but according to
Maka, the Eridani got around. Their folk had all kinds of
spacefaring capabilities. They were kind of like the pirate
mercenaries of our galaxy. They hadn't made the acquaintance of any of the Powers That Be on Earth yet,
Maka thought, because we neither had anything they
wanted nor presented them with any kind of unmanagea-
ble threat. That probably wouldn't always be the case, but
for the moment anyway, our solar system was low on
their list of piratey targets.

Lucky us.

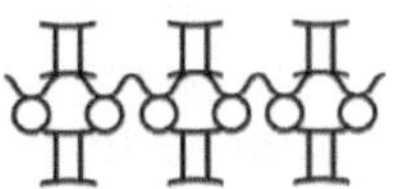

THE LAST TIME we went up against the Eridani we
didn't have the suits, and it didn't go so well.

That time, a year ago, Rakow and Shadow were doing their regular check of campus, camouflaged as the
typical evening dog walk. Cold rain was just beginning to
spit here and there when Shadow alerted to a scent in the
grass, and with Rakow on his heels, tracked it to the
maintenance building – or The Smokestack as it was

generally called.

Concealed under an overhang near the trash bins at the back of the building, Rakow and Shadow spotted the first Eridani. It had been badly injured, probably from its unexpected journey through the Portal from wherever the wormhole's tail was flailing at that moment to here. I spared little sympathy for the creature, though. First, because even injured, the Eridani were way too badass to be pitiable, and second, because the first thing it did was attack Shadow.

Eridani were large, easily seven feet tall. Despite their size, they were masters of camouflage. The one that had attacked Jen back on the In-Between planet where we'd rescued Barb and Alesta, had concealed itself in plain sight on some sandy, rocky ground. This one had been so badly injured that its ability to conceal itself was on the fritz. It was mostly visible where it sprawled, leaking its alien fluids onto the concrete pad under the trash bins. Stinking, acidic smoke rose wherever the creature's blood or venom, whatever it was dripped, and it ate the cement away.

Shadow approached cautiously, but the tentacles were faster and longer than he expected and before Rakow could catch up to him, the Eridani had flicked out one long tentacle, gripped Shadow with those venomous suckers and tossed him ten feet away, both dog and attacker screaming in pain. Rakow saw it happen and rushed in. The injured Eridani hissed and flailed at him, but this time, it kept its tentacles under the overhang, out of the cold, blustery rain.

Mr. Rakow was always armed with something or other. In fact, one of his favorite pastimes was creating new and ingenious weaponry that was made specifically for the kinds of hinky bad guys we specialized in.

He saw the smoking holes the creature's blood was making in the concrete pad, and he was no fool. If this thing had something toxic for blood, he wasn't about to shoot more holes in it. Instead, he pulled a sticky bomb from his tool belt. He'd been modifying his sticky bombs since way back when we blew up Charlie Starkweather's 1949 ghost Ford in the junior high school hallway on Halloween. While the explosive in those sticky bombs was a bunch of M-80 fireworks, these guys were more complex. Working with Pat, they'd created an implosive sticky blob that was packed with little balls of something that had started off as white phosphorous. However, where our old friend Willy Pete needed oxygen to burn, these just needed a magic word to ignite and then they consumed whatever organic matter they touched completely.

Mr. Rakow shouted the magic words, *Cinis Cinerem!* and tossed two sticky bombs at the Eridani. It tried to bat away the first one, but of course the little bomb did its job and stuck to the Eridani's tentacle. The second one Rakow lobbed hit center mass. What was left of that Eridani by the time we arrived was a ball of goop about the size of a lunchbox.

He rushed over to Shadow and radioed for help on the handheld my dad had gifted him for Christmas. That still might have been too late, had Jen's vision of an injured Shadow not tipped us off ahead of time. Mom and I were already on our way.

The amount of Eridani toxin Shadow had absorbed into his 90-pound frame was profound. He was unconscious when we arrived, just seconds after Rakow's radio call for help. It took both Mom's and my healing magic together to save him. Rakow knelt by Shadow's side while we worked, looking like he, himself might explode or collapse at any second. I don't think he even breathed until he saw Shadow's tail give a slow, thumping wag.

Rakow gave my mom and then me a look of extreme gratitude, took Shadow's head in his hands, kissed his head and whispered a few words before saying aloud, "You stay here with Doc Parsons now, buddy. I'll be right back." Then he straightened up and strode over to join the war council Maka, David, Jen and my dad were holding a few yards away.

"They travel in threes," Maka told the group. "If the other two survived the trip through the wormhole, they'll either go to ground someplace nearby, or they'll be on the run. We have to find them."

Just then, Lorraine, Diane, Becky and Rome appeared. Diane and Rome were carrying garden tools, and Becky was hauling the heavy metal box we used to transport alien goop out to Maka's place for disposal.

"Sounds like you need a tracking spell," Becky said, dropping the metal box by the trash bins and joining the council. "Are there any bits left of that thing I can use for the spell?"

"Over here!" Diane called. She held a shovel on which sat a clump of grass, burned at the top, but healthy at the bottom, ready to go into the metal box. Perched atop the smoldering mass was a little chunk of tentacle.

*Ew*

Within a few minutes, Becky's spell pegged the remaining two creatures about a mile away, at Snyder industries. Right next to the train tracks.

"We need to get to them before they can hop a train and get out of town," Mr. Rakow said, looking at his watch.

We ran. We found them, and we brought them down, but it was an ugly fight against smart and well-armed enemies. Both Rakow and I got shot. Me in the hip, him in the shoulder, near his heart. The bolts didn't make holes the way bullets did, instead they operated on some vibrational level that disrupted our mechanical functioning.

When I got hit, my legs went numb and stayed that way for nearly 12 hours before the pain even started. The paralysis was rotten. The pain was worse. Even Mom's best continued efforts to heal our injuries only yielded partial results. I limped and Rakow grumbled about his arm for months before we were more or less back to normal.

Mom cautioned Rakow repeatedly that the shot he'd taken had done some serious damage to his heart. She warned him that it needed time and more gentle exercise than he normally practiced in order to heal up properly.

If Rakow was dismissive of Mom's medical advice, David wasn't. He was more subtle about it though, tying it in with Shadow's recovery from the Eridani toxin. Even with our magical help, the experience had been a severe one for the aging dog. David assured Lorraine he was watching Rakow closely when the two of them were alone, doing their usual runs and workouts. If Shadow tired out, David insisted Rakow slow down to match his dog's pace. Over the past year, David and Rakow had become pretty much inseparable.

While Rakow wouldn't ever admit weakness, with some nudges from Mom and Lorraine, he begrudgingly bowed to the idea that he had to be in good, healthy shape to look out for Shadow and David, who both needed him immensely. In the end, the experience changed bonds that were strong into bonds that were unbreakable.

I think that's partly why Mike's appearance hit Rakow as hard as it did.

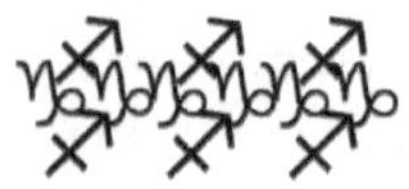

I HAD JEN'S coverall inspected and ready for her to slip on the minute she parked Clint on campus. As we drew nearer, we passed progressively more people on foot. A lot of them were dressed in brightly colored outfits that gleamed hopefully under street lights against the cold, grey night.

"So, what did you think of Mike?" I asked, shuttling the thought of rainbow clad party guests aside. Jen looked both ways and then ran the red light at 56th St.

"He's great, but not great for David," she said thoughtfully.

"What do you mean?" I asked.

"I mean, David needs a dad. You've always had yours. I mean no offense by that, Ang, this isn't a dig, but you don't know exactly how it feels to not have one around. I sort of do. He's been better, recently you know, since he got his job and house situation figured out. He does his best to be around when we need him, these days, but it wasn't always like that.

I knew this to be true. There had been more than one occasion when questions or difficulties had come up for Jon, when Lorraine just hadn't had the right kind of answers. Jon had a pretty good relationship with his dad now, good enough so that when those things popped up, he didn't hesitate to get on the phone and get their dad's take on things. That's not to say he always took his dad's advice, but it was there for him, and he factored it in.

My dad was a big star in my sky, but I understood that he wasn't exactly the dad David needed, either. Mr. Rakow, on the other hand, truly was. They had bonded early on, when David was little and Mr. Rakow lived next door, and that bond had grown by leaps and bounds after Mitch and Donna's accident. Rakow and David had so much in common; their love of dogs, outdoor adventures, military type strategies and weapons. Because of David, Rakow had even become a die-hard Star Wars fan. They'd spend whole weekends sometimes watching all three movies back-to-back on video cassette.

"Don't get me wrong, I think Mike's probably pretty freaking wonderful. In fact, I think that's a big part of the reason he's so great at what he does. With that face and his ability to share emotions, he's exactly what they need to gather followers and get something done. But from what I can tell, he's geared differently. Maybe he is an Inorog, like Jon says. If he is, if that story is true, people like that can get completely bound up by their connection to other people. It's like they *live* for others. Literally.

"David needs someone who is totally present in the real world. Totally grounded. Someone who can teach him about the real nitty gritty stuff, not someone who is floating away on everyone else's thoughts and feelings all the time, you know?" She turned the corner onto Huntington and into one of the diagonal parking spots alongside the football field.

She killed Clint's engine and lights, and slid over to the middle spot in the front seat. She took her coverall from my outstretched hand, and started suiting up. What she said made sense.

I thought back to our experiences with Mitch. Had David been only in tune to what Mitch was feeling, he may have had a better understanding of what made Mitch tick, but he probably wouldn't have learned how to protect himself from it.

It was Rakow who'd built up David's confidence,

who'd drilled it into his head that it wasn't his fault when Mitch doled out the abuse. He'd given David a clearer perspective of the situation, and shown David by example how to stand up to bullies.

Jen zipped up her coverall and started checking her weapons. "Remember that thing you were telling us about after you read *The Stand*? How that one character was, what did you say, something about *other—*?"

I cast back in my mind for what long-winded book reviews I'd given Jen, trying to get her to read Stephen King's 800+ page book about plague and evil. "Other directed?" I asked, attaching my crossbow to its shoulder harness.

"Yeah. Other directed. Like, she was great, but she wasn't practical. She got the survivors to Colorado and all that, but she was zero help organizing a new society. She was totally wrapped up in her relationship with her God. That was who she was listening to and who called her shots."

"You think he's not calling his own shots?" I asked.

"Yeah." Jen said. "I think that. I think he's all wrapped up in Jim. I think Mike's great guy, maybe a super gifted Inorog, but probably totally impractical, and I'm betting," she tightened her boot lace with a sharp tug and said in a brusque tone, "totally untrustworthy."

*Yikes.*

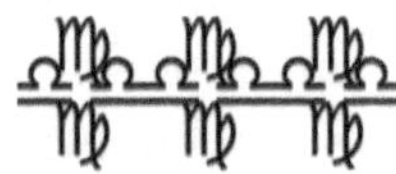

WE EMERGED FROM Clint into the cold night air. Behind us, across the street, lights and music spilled from one of the big old houses that had been chopped up into student apartments. A flag in rainbow colors was stuck outside the open door, from which we could hear the musical stylings of George Michael.

In front of us, the lights on campus looked slightly wavery. I knew this was the result of the outer ring of protection spells the Coven had in place. Their regular daily spells only covered the immediate area around the Portal, everything else on campus was rigged to permit normal access by students and staff.

Maka had kicked the spells into their highest gear, the level reserved for imminent threats. In this configuration, they would block not only outside spellcasters, like the witches the Pilgrims had on their side, but they also made a physical boundary. We'd had years to plan for this moment. We were as ready as we could possibly be, and yet, Rakow's words haunted me. "A plan is only as good as first contact."

We had drawn our line in the sand, and the Pilgrims had come to bust it up. From here on out, it was up to us to adapt to whatever they threw at us. Everything we knew, everything we'd learned, all of it was in play starting now.

I spotted a black and white cruiser and waved at Office Yardley as he passed. He'd been thoroughly briefed about all our precautions, and knew to keep his team outside the first barrier. I wasn't sure how much of a police presence we could expect, I guess that depended on how many folks on the force he felt could be trusted with this, and how many Pilgrims attempted to cross the boundary and wound up sick, injured or unconscious outside it. He gave his red lights a quick flash in return and continued his slow circle of campus.

Jen and I strode through the first spell boundary,

feeling the tug of resistance and release. The spell knew us, and it let us through because we were equipped with the *key*. Not a real key, of course, but a magical one that identified the Guardian, the Triad, Maka and her clan, the Healer, the Coven and of course Jon, Rakow and the dogs.

Anyone else trying to enter campus right now would first be hit with a powerful feeling that they were needed somewhere else. Anywhere else but here. Maka had let us feel the effects of these spells before equipping us with our keys, and they were mega-intense. For my part, I was flat out convinced that our house was on fire and Bast was trapped in the secret room. I was halfway home at full tilt before Barb caught me and stopped me.

The second line of defense on that outer spell was more physical. It created pain sensations in the brain of anyone trying to enter. David bravely volunteered to try that one out, and he was on his knees in seconds, holding his head and barfing with what he described later as a totally killer migraine.

Anyone who endured those first two effects was then rendered terribly confused. That one took a while to wear off, too. It was like, three hours before Jen could even remember her own name after she experienced that one.

That was just the outer boundary. There were two more inside that one before you got to the portal. Maka and the Coven didn't fool around.

Once we were inside, we were hit with our first sense of how weird everything had become. From outside, other than the slight wonkiness of the lights, campus looked pretty normal. In here, it was a different story.

The ghastly smell hit me first. It was like burning rubber mixed with ammonia. Jen and I donned our full-face masks immediately and helped one another seal them to our coveralls. We looked a little like some kind of early 60's Astronaut Barbie with them on, but boy they did the trick. That smell was neutralized immediately and we could breathe normally right away.

Dad and Rakow had rigged the suits with radio capabilities, and even gone so far as to create our own little pirate station, but we'd discovered while testing the suits around magic that it sometimes futzed with the reception, even when we were at close range. Dad's solution to that was that we all learn Morse code so if all we could hear was static, there was still a chance we could communicate with dits and dahs tapped out with a button installed inside the glove of the coverall.

- . - - . - - . - - / . . - . . .

"Can you hear me, Jen?" I asked, hoping we could get away with voice communication for a while at least before resorting to that.

"Roger," Jen replied.

Okay. Some static, but okay. We high fived and started the quick jog over to Old Main. The thirteen Coven members were already taking their assigned places within that first circle of protection. We waved at Ginny as we jogged past. She sat lotus-style on one of the topmost bleachers at the southeast corner of the football field. Her red hair was braided tightly against her skull so it would fit underneath her face mask. She gave us a thumbs-up as we ran by.

The four cardinal directions were held by the four most experienced witches; Dot on the south, Lorraine on the north, Rome on the east side and Pat on the west. Nicole and Lisa were evenly spaced along the northwest curve of the circle, Becky and Diane were on the northeast, Jules, Deanne and Miss Charlotte who had filled

Shelly's place as the newest member took the southwest, and Elizabeth and Ginny took the southeast. Mom was positioned between Lorraine and Lisa, suited up and loaded with first aid of the physical and the magical variety. She was our one-woman medical team.

I sent up a little wish with the hope that she would be unneeded, and followed it up with one hoping that if she was, she would be fast, effective and safe.

Guarding the second defensive spell would be Maka, Barb, Malinowski and Rakow. If anyone got through that first outer circle, they'd be flanked by witches to their rear, and warriors ahead of them. Anyone able to get past that formidable resistance would be met by the second circle, the one we called *The Moat*. It was, among other things, a visual spell that gave the appearance of a bottomless chasm.

Without the key to that one, if you tried to step or jump or even fly over it, you would first experience what it was like to fall into a bottomless pit for several terrifying minutes that felt more like an hour, only to find yourself flat on your back outside the first spell wall where you started. If you were lucky, you landed unconscious. If you were unlucky, you landed semi-lucid, beset by terrifying visions rockslides, avalanches, or sometimes drowning. That part had Pat's fingerprints all over it, but she got plenty of help from Deanne and Elizabeth.

One practice trip through that particular thrill ride was more than enough for me. Even knowing full well that I was totally suited up and keyed to cross *The Moat*, I did it with my eyes closed. It was just too freaky.

As Jen and I made our way in, the radio was busy with people checking in to their positions. The only one outside the circle at this point was going to be Jon, who was at home, acting as our communications hub. He not only kept track of all our radio transmissions, but in the event that all radio communications went down, Jon could mentally *piggyback* in on any one of us, relaying information to whoever needed it most.

The dogs were free to roam throughout the campus as they were needed. Their harnesses were keyed to all three spell walls, and they were practiced enough to understand that they could maneuver around any of them safely. I say practiced enough, and that was true, but without David's ability to reassure and teach them, I don't think they'd have been as cavalier about it as they were. He told them they were safe, and they believed him.

The third and innermost circle was the simplest and strongest spell. It wasn't just a circle surrounding the Portal, it was an entire sphere. This spell relied almost entirely on magically concentrated blunt force, and was as much intended to keep Pilgrims out as it was to keep whatever hinkiness was coming out of the portal in. Clara Mills' ghost was also present, and also able to cross all the spell walls, although being non-corporeal, she mostly stayed close the Portal as things like poison gas and gravity wells didn't bother her at all.

Guarding that innermost circle were me, David, Jen, and the Guardian. We were the last line of defense against full scale chaos. But first, we had to get there. Several hundred yards in front of us, on the east side of the Smokestack, sat the Student Center. Or it used to, anyway.

The ground beneath my feet moved. This, I can assure you, is a confusing and frightening sensation. I came to a totally involuntary stop next to Jen and looked at her, wide eyed through my face mask. Then the earth opened up 30 yards in front of us and took the Student Center. Glass shattered, pipes screamed, fires sprouted, bricks crashed. The ground shook again and we fell to our hands and knees. Voices exploded in our headsets.

"What was that??"

"Earthquake! The Student Center collapsed!"

"Lorraine! Becky! Diane! Check in!"

"Here!"

"Safe!"

"Yee haw!" shouted Becky. I caught a glimpse of her levitating over the mass of demolished stone and exposed pipes.

"Check the perimeter!"

"Spellmarkers are intact!"

"Outer layer solid!"

Jen and I got to our feet and took off again, bearing slightly left to avoid a fallen light pole that used to illuminate the walking path here under the trees. The trees were swaying, but none had fallen yet. Over the radio chatter I could hear more crashes as the Student Center, now behind us, continued to transform into its new configuration. Ruin.

We ran on.

We quickly approached *The Moat* without breaking stride. The appearance of the enormous hole in the ground was no less disconcerting than ever. I squeezed my eyes shut and kept running. The second I opened my eyes after crossing, I saw Shadow and Tati bounding towards us. Their spellwork head protection glimmered slightly like almost totally clear glass fishbowls around their heads. Their barking was slightly quieter than normal, but their grins were undiminished. My heart gave a joyous thump. Our good dogs joined us as we ran.

Rakow jogged smartly past us on his way to his position.

"Keep your eyes open, your heads on a swivel, and

remember your training!" he shouted. We saluted him and kept going.

And then we stopped, and looked up. I'm sure my mouth was hanging open.

The Guardian and David met us there at the boundary of the sphere around the Portal. Dad checked the seal on David's helmet and clapped him on the back. David gave him a thumbs up then turned to us and winked. He had his game face on, keenly alert and fierce. Clara was hovering just inside the spell wall with her hands up, indicating that we should come no farther. I was happy to comply.

The Portal had become completely unhinged. Inside the sphere where the old Music Building used to be, in between Old Main, the Admin building and Olin Science Hall there now appeared a massive storm. Lightning flashed, flames erupted here and there, and something that looked like a firehose made of black nothingness flailed around wildly, its one end a giant maw opening and closing, its other end a tiny pinprick of blackness that seemed to come from nowhere.

For the moment, the storm and the flailing portal were contained inside a complicated structure of spells. Talk about a tempest in a teapot. Clara's ghostly figure swayed inside the barrier. As we watched, horrified, a shower of boulders exploded out the maw of the portal, pelting the interior of the spell wall. I flinched back, instinctively, but for now, anyway, the spell wall held.

I felt the blood drain from my face. I looked at my dad.

"That's what they want? That's what the Pilgrims want to dive into?" I asked, aghast.

Dad shook his head, his face full of compassion and resolve. "That's what a desperate heart can make you believe, and there's nothing more dangerous than a true believer in possession of a lie," he said.

"And we have to keep them out of there," David said, his amber eyes slanted under his furrowed brow. "In order to protect the balance of matter in the universe."

"That is our mission," Dad said.

"For how long?" Jen asked.

"Until the Portal collapses," he replied.

"How long will that be?" I asked.

"If we're lucky, not very long," he replied with a small smile.

*Oh boy.*

"We've got company over here, guys," came Rome's voice over the radio.

David, Jenny, Dad and I nodded sharply at one another and took our positions around the portal.

"How many?" Rakow asked.

"Half a dozen," she replied. "They're gathering around the outer spell wall. Heh, two of them just ran off in a panic."

That meant the spell was working. I wondered what was on fire for those folks.

"We've got a couple of cars pulling up on the north side," came Lorraine's voice.

"Here too, south side, three cars and a van," Dot said.

"Three grown men in very tight jeans running as fast as they can away from my location," Miss Charlotte said, her voice tight with adrenaline, but she also sounded amused. I grinned just a little.

"A black and white just stopped a big group of people across the street over here on the northwest," Nicole said. "They all look really confused. The officer is directing them away from the campus. Guys, are we sure these people are dangerous? All the people in this group looked like they were dressed for a Pride event."

I thought back to the groups of brightly dressed people we'd seen on the way here.

Jen's voice came over the radio, "We saw a party with a rainbow flag out front happening just off campus, over on the south side, close to 56th."

Great. That's just what this situation called for. Innocent bystanders. Officer Yardley and his team were going to have their hands full.

A moment later, Pat's low, gravelly voice intoned, "Three, wait…four busses just parked in front of the sorority on 50th street.

*Busses? Oh crap.*

"Yep, they're packed full, too. Fifty or sixty getting off each one," said Jules.

"More Pride partiers?" Nicole asked.

"Not this group," Jules said. "I'm seeing walking staves and hooded cloaks. They seem organized, and they're headed this way."

Jon's voice came over the radio then, "Guys, they're coming at you from every direction. Hundreds of people. I can sense them all the way from here. Their auras are weird. Some of them are very focused, but some of them seem sort of confused, maybe drugged or bespelled, I can't tell. And they're all following directions from somebody. Someone, I think, in a vehicle. They're parked on the south side, Dorothy, nearest your position."

"I see it, Jon. It's that white van," Dottie replied calmly. "People in cloaks are coming up to the driver's side and talking to someone through the window."

"And here come the witches, y'all!" Ginny's voice sounded a little wild in my ears. "Rome, honey, you see 'em? Three groups of three, across the street and to your left!"

"Yeah, baby!" Rome sang out. "Buckle up, everybody!"

"Focus, Coven!" Came Lorraine's voice. "Our job is to maintain that outer boundary spell for as long as we possibly can. Nobody gets to go rogue here, we need everyone to stay on point! If you need directed spell fire, call for one of the dogs. They're mobile and can get in location to direct spells out. Watch your sisters, conserve your energy, and keep your heads. It might be a long night."

For the next hour or so, the Coven worked to keep the boundary strong, and Shadow, Tati and Alesta moved about strategically, activating spells to discourage groups of witches gathering outside the barrier and receiving treats for jobs well done. Their harness arsenals included spells that sent blasts of magically disruptive sound, crazy lights and fireworks out through the spell walls to undo or at least upset whatever spellcasting was going on just outside. Wherever a group of three in cloaks gathered, the witch on that section of the circle would call for canine intervention.

Jon told me later that David was carefully visualizing the witch that needed help and sending that to Tati or Shadow. They would take that image and go galivanting off to which witch was which who would trigger the appropriate spell remotely, and then give the dog a good pet and a cookie. The dogs were having a blast.

Jon reported to all of us that people kept arriving all around campus, despite the police presence in the neighborhood. The witches on the perimeter were reporting more and more groups of people dressed in all sorts of wild costumes, some with crazy high heels and wigs, others with feathered capes and brightly colored hair. And moving amongst them were increasing numbers of people wearing drab brown cloaks with hoods.

Dot's voice came over the radio, calm and alert. "Focus on the ones in the cloaks, witches, but keep your eyes peeled. The Pride party may be just a distraction, but I just saw a couple of drag queens talking to the people in the white van. Whatever is going on, it all seems to be connected."

Rakow, Maka, Malinowski and Barb walked back and forth on their portions of The Moat, watching for anything or anyone that might have gotten through the perimeter. David, Jen, Dad and I paced around the interior spell wall, keeping an eye on its strength, and watching the Portal flail and grow and spit stuff out. There was water, then fire, then some kind of purple goo, several things that looked sort of like aquatic dinosaurs, a flock of something similar to the big leathery bat things we'd seen once before, and clouds of noxious looking gasses. Sometimes it sucked everything back in and the maw became tinier and tinier, just to expand again and belch something new out.

All the grass and trees and soil inside the sphere had been utterly destroyed, along with whatever infrastructure ran underground that space. The grounds crew was going to have a conniption fit when they saw it. If they saw it. Nervous acid chewed at my stomach. Jon popped in periodically to check on me and the Portal.

"Hundreds of people are milling around campus and the neighborhood." Jon said from inside my head, a sensation that had long since stopped feeling odd. "Groups that get too close to the boundary get repelled, and then another group will wander up. Yardley and his officers are circling, directing confused people away but there are just too many to keep track of."

The night was dark and cold, and clouds gathered

overhead.

Officer Yardley, who had our private radio channel came on around 1:00 a.m. and said, "We've blocked off the streets around campus. No more cars are allowed in. Official report is that someone invited a bunch of people to a rave and it got out of control. But there are so many people already in the area on foot now, we don't have enough officers to keep all of them away from the barrier. Several homes and vehicles in the immediate area have been broken into. Homeowners are having confrontations with people on their lawns. We've requested more backup, but the Chief is dragging his feet. We'll keep you posted. Yardley out."

In the end, it was a fatal combination of things occurring simultaneously that ended the stalemate. I'm not sure what kind of vision alerted Jen, but all we got was about a five second notice when her voice came over the radio, a little breathlessly.

"Heads up everybody! Here we go!"

The ground rumbled under my feet. It's an unnerving feeling. I mean, the ground doesn't just move like that. Or it shouldn't, anyway. In my humble opinion. It's just totally messed up.

I threw my arms out and tried to keep my balance. A big, dark crack zigzagged across the ground between me and the Theater building on the south side of campus. By big I mean about five feet wide and who knew how deep. I scuttled backwards to get away from it. It ran directly towards the building. For a second, I thought maybe it had stopped, and then another big shake rattled my brains, and the Theater building split in two.

"Spellmarker down!" Dottie's radio voice cut through my shock.

The spellmarkers were the physical grounding points

of the spells. They were located inside the outer barrier, all around the campus. Each witch was positioned near one, and had been continually feeding it with her power now for hours. If one of them went down, it wasn't a complete catastrophe. The circle of magic was more like a web, so if one point failed, the others could take up the slack. It would take five or six of them going down at once to completely destabilize the boundary spell.

"Here too! Marker down!" Elizabeth's voice.

"Crap!" shouted Jules. Their witches have taken over the sorority house. They're attacking the spell wall here! It's about to go!"

"Breach! Breach! Breach!" shouted Deanne.

That only left Miss Charlotte, the newest member of the Coven and least experienced witch holding the line on the south side.

"Back Charlotte up!" Lorraine shouted; the strain evident in her voice. "Witches! Back Charlotte up!"

I was on my feet and in position, my head on a swivel, like Mr. Rakow had taught us. I could feel the magical strain in the air, in my head, in my heart. C'mon, witches! C'mon, Miss Charlotte! Hang in there!!

And then I heard, Malinowski shout, "Frickin' Eridani!"

At the same moment Barb sang out, "Two Eridani! South door! Old Main!"

*Crap!*

Barb and Malinowski were on opposite sides of Old Main. If they were both seeing Eridani that meant they'd come out of both sides of the building.

Then I heard a sound that made my heart almost stop. It was a big, deep cracking sound, not like glass cracking, or wood. More like what I imagined the Titanic might have sounded like when it hit that iceberg. A huge, sharp, crack.

I swiveled my head to look at the sphere around the Portal. A crack was forming about twenty feet above my head, and running down, down, down the south side. A funny whistling sound came out of it, like the air leaking out of a very large metal balloon.

Then I heard a sound I knew very well from living my whole life in northeast Lincoln, home of the muscle car and its attendant gear-head. It was the sound of a motor revving along with tires spinning. Someone was accelerating rapidly with the brakes on. Once they released the brake, whatever vehicle that was would take off at a very high speed.

"The van!" Dottie shouted. "Hold the line, witches! Hold the line!"

"I'm losing it! Oh, goddess, I'm losing it!" came Miss Charlotte's anguished cry.

The van released its brakes. It came flying at the south spell wall, in between Charlotte and Deanne's positions, and boom, it was through and flying across campus at breakneck speed.

In between the van and my position guarding the sphere, was *The Moat*. It was powered by a different set of spellmarkers, fed mainly by Maka, who was now holding off the Eridani that had been hiding in Old Main. If she could maintain the spellmarkers long enough for the Coven to switch their focus from the south side web to her, we had a chance.

I heard the descending screams of a dozen or so robed fools who attempted the leap across *The Moat* ahead of the onrushing van, and I imagined the thumps they'd make when they got spit back out on the sidewalk off campus. There was something sort of Monte Python's Flying Circus about the whole thing, but I felt no desire to laugh. Behind me, the ground rumbled again.

*CRAP!*

This earthquake took out the two spellmarkers on the north side of *The Moat*. Just sucked them right down into the ground. It held for a second longer, and then the whole spell collapsed. The van, as though its driver had planned his roaring approach right down to the millisecond, flew over the space recently occupied by a magical hole in the ground, and crashed at full speed into the already-weakened spell wall around the Portal.

I caught a glimpse of driver and passenger being flung hard against their seatbelts, and once again heard that cracking sound before I was surrounded by cloaked Pilgrims.

My crossbow was loaded with arrows that were made especially for this particular task. The arrows themselves were blunt. Getting hit directly in the chest with one of them hurt like blue blazes, but it didn't penetrate the skin. What it did do, was release a cloud of sleeping gas. It only took a breath or two of the stuff before you were down for the count. Since all of us were masked up, they were an excellent crowd deterrent. Six fast shots later and instead of facing a group of thirty crazed looking Pilgrims, I was looking at a pile of thirty sleeping Pilgrims. Unfortunately, there was another crowd rushing up behind them.

*CRAP*

The radio was ablaze with reports from all over campus. I tried to listen with half my brain while the other half shot until I was out of arrows. I dropped my crossbow and began hurling bespelled grenades which exploded in a variety of ways, from sonic blasts to tiny darts that delivered more knockout juice while also incapacitating arms and legs. Still, they kept coming. They were running over their fellow Pilgrims, all of them absolutely intent on reaching the Portal.

I still to this day can't watch movies about the Zombie apocalypse. I just can't.

"Behind you, Jules!"

"Eridani in the weeds, Barb, look out!"

"Pilgrims coming over the hedge!"

"Pat! On your left!"

The Coven witches were retreating towards us, some of them casting spells right and left with wands and staves, others going in for hand to hand using bespelled blades. Elizabeth was wielding her pen, a wild magical weapon of her own design. With it she could create illusions real enough to give you nightmares. Aiming toward one cluster of approaching Pilgrims she quickly sketched in the air the shape of a bull with long horns, which promptly burst into being and chased them helter skelter off campus the way they'd come. Next was a winged lion followed by a bonfire with legs. Pilgrims fled at her approach.

Deanne was surrounded by blue waves of magic that stopped anyone from getting within fifteen feet of her. She'd based that spell on a creature called a Hagfish. The waves, if they got into your eyes or mouth, would fill you up with your own mucus. If you were fond of breathing or seeing, you had no choice but to stop and spit, scratch and claw the stuff out of your eyes and airway. Gross, and super effective.

I heard, rather than saw Becky go howling past, which meant she was under an invisibility spell, and most likely, airborne. A rain of stinging pellets followed in her wake, causing any Pilgrims in that path to fall about themselves like they'd been beset by hornets.

I heard a series of really concentrated explosions followed by the distinctly high-pitched screams of an injured

Eridani from somewhere behind me. David and Rakow must have brought along the Jarts from Rakow's arsenal. Before the Coven got hold of them, Jarts were a merely mega-dangerous, *very* occasionally fatal lawn dart game popular for a minute in the 1980s before being banned. Afterwards, they were worse. Much worse. At least, if you were an Eridani.

Pat and Becky had worked up a potent mix of the same implosive sticky goo from their already fatal sticky bombs, with a freezing potion, and loaded it into the nose of the dart. The result was a blue plastic thing that looked kind of like a lethal bomb pop with deadly aim that when it encountered Eridani flesh or venom, froze it solidly to absolute zero and then imploded it. Apparently, it was devastatingly effective. I heard the distinctive scream and crunch one more time. Two down, one to go.

Another booming crack sounded from the sphere around the Portal, and the whole top blew off of it. I spun to look, terrified what I might see.

The Portal flailed upwards and then flipped down, like an angry snake seeking prey. It shattered the remaining walls of the containment spell and what had a second ago seemed like chaos, now seemed like an afternoon at the park.

All around us, cloaked Pilgrims dropped to their knees and started chanting in a kind of worshipful reverence. Those further away ran closer, weeping and wailing.

The maw of the portal pointed groundward. I didn't notice the sudden lack of oxygen, since I was still sealed up inside my coverall, but the nearby Pilgrims did. The ones closest to the Portal grabbed at their throats. The Portal flipped and flailed again, and two or three people who'd just been standing maybe thirty feet away from me were sucked in. They were there one second, and then the next, they were down the Portal's gullet.

"Retreat! Retreat!" Rakow was screaming in my ears. I was never so happy to follow an order in my entire life. I backed away, dodging the Pilgrims who were still running forward. I could hear them coughing and gasping the nearer they got to the thin air around portal. More and more Pilgrims fell to their knees. From behind me the chanting grew louder.

Then the portal's maw began spitting stuff out again. A huge gout of flame incinerated the group of Pilgrims who had gathered on the east side of it. More rushed up to take their places. It was insanity.

"Witches! Regroup at Old Main!" Dottie and Lorraine were trying to corral the Coven. They seemed to be trying to reestablish the containment spell around the Portal. I couldn't tell how many of the Coven were able to even get over there.

Very calmly and quietly in my head came Jon's voice. "Ang, you three need to try to contain it until the Coven can get their spell recast. David's in position on the west side, Jen can take the south if you can get around on to the northeast."

"Which way? Where?" I was already moving.

"Just a little further, head toward the smokestack. There, okay, fire it up."

I reached one arm out in Jen's direction, the other toward David and the stones did their thing. I honestly didn't think we could be enough, not enough to contain this massive beast of a thing. It belched lightning and a chunk of what looked like an iceberg came flying out of it, followed by a gout of sand. The iceberg crashed into Old Main, right where the Coven had gathered and sand all but buried the white van that had rammed the barrier spell.

I wanted to scream and cry and run, but I didn't. Jon's voice in my head quieted all my thoughts and I focused entirely on making that connection with David and Jenny and holding it tight. We were together, all of us. We were holding the line. Our perimeter was large enough to encompass the whole Portal along with whatever else happened to be nearby, including the van.

The sense of rightness, of wholeness that I always felt when David, Jen and I were connected this way filled me. For a moment, I felt like we could hold this thing. I really did, and then it flailed again and I was lifted clean up off my feet. Before I had time to panic, I was caught by friendly hands, and gently set back down.

"Don't worry, Ang," came Becky's disembodied voice midair. "I got you."

I felt suddenly grounded and strong. I felt arms around me and heard my dad's voice, whether it was over the radio or just in my head, there was too much going on for me to know for sure, but it was his voice.

"We can do this, sweetie," Dad said.

The light formed by the connection of our living stone necklaces swelled then, bolstered by the power of the Guardian and fueled by the magic of whatever members of the Coven were still casting. I couldn't tell if it was all of them, but I really, really hoped it was.

The Pilgrims trying to reach the Portal were unable to cross the barrier made by our light. They screamed and cried and pounded their fists against the wall of energy we were holding. The maw sucked sharply back, so far back I thought for a second it might actually close, and then it whirled and dove again, open as wide as I'd seen it yet.

That's when the passenger door of the van was kicked open from the inside, and Mike stumbled out.

*Oh Crap!*

He barely gave the looming mouth hanging over his head a second glance. Instead, he sprinted around the back end of the mangled Astro Van. He wrenched open the driver's side door and started to pull his friend Jim out. The impact of the crash had evidently rattled Jim's skull because he wasn't looking too great.

*Oh, Crap!*

It flooded over me. This was why Jim had brought Mike to Lincoln! Jim was a Pilgrim, and by the looks of it, he was the *head* Pilgrim. He'd organized this whole thing in tandem with the group of Pride activists heading for DC. All these people, the activists, the witches, the Pilgrims, he'd set this all into motion.

And Mike had gone along with it because he was emotionally bound to Jim, and so he believed what Jim believed – that this was his miracle. This was what would cure him of AIDS.

And now there they were, exactly where they wanted to be, about to be sucked into an interspatial wormhole to who knows where. To be totally honest, I didn't really care all that much about Jim. He was a grown man who could make his own fool choices. In fact, if he'd truly been responsible for convincing all these people that they should follow him, then to heck with him. He could go. Good riddance.

But Mike was David's dad. The dad he never even knew about and had met for all of two hours and really liked. Mike was, by all accounts, a really good, if foolish, guy. Mike didn't deserve this; he didn't deserve to be dragged to his inevitable death because he was all wrapped up in Jim's drama.

Mike's gift of extreme empathy had really steered him wrong with Jim. I just bet Jim knew that. I bet Jim knew he had a good thing going when he roped Mike in, with his ready-made group of followers, all desperate for a miracle. I just bet that Mike was being badly used, and that knowledge hurt my heart.

The Portal whirled again, almost disappearing and then reappearing, this time with a maw full of lava.

"Dad!" screamed David.

Mike looked just in time and pushed Jim back inside the van. He jumped in on top of him and closed the door. Lava hit the ground just in front of the van and splattered the hood and windshield. It pooled up all around the walls we were holding and encircled the van. Then the Portal zipped back inside itself again leaving a tiny burning pinprick of black flame hovering a dozen or so feet overhead.

"You've got to get out of there!" David yelled. I felt the tug of his side of the triad as he took a rushing step towards the van. "The Portal is unstable! You'll die!"

"No!" Jen yelled. "David, don't let go, you can't!"

If David dropped his end, if he made an opening, the still boiling pool of lava would rush out, incinerating him and a couple dozen more Pilgrims who were bowing and praying or banging on the force field, trying to get in.

Mike cranked the driver's side window down halfway, eyeing the ground below. The lava had pooled all around the van at this point. The wheels were on fire. The van was sinking, slowly. There was no way they could get out now, even if they wanted to.

That's when Becky threw off the invisibility spell she'd been wearing and flew over to where Rakow stood, just outside the barrier. She actually had a broom. I couldn't believe it! Of all the times for Becky to go traditional. I'd have thought for sure if she was going to bewitch something to fly around on, it would have been a Stratocaster or a Flying V. Go figure.

She zoomed over to where Rakow stood. Over the radio I heard her say to him, "If you can grab him out of there, I can fly us out!"

"How will you get us through the barrier?" Rakow asked. Oh crap, he was actually on board for this crazy plan!

"With this," Becky held up the chunk of meteor that had come from our friend Callean, the space dwelling creature of living stone, same as our necklaces. "It's keyed to the same frequency as their necklaces. It should let us through and back!"

"Rakow, no!" David moaned; his fists clenched.

"I can save him!" Rakow shouted.

"It can't work! You'll never make it out alive!" Lorraine yelled at Becky.

"Look!" someone else shouted. The Portal was glowing blindingly white hot and expanding again.

"If we're going, we need to go now!" Becky said urgently.

The van tires exploded then, and the van dropped several more inches down into the pool of lava. The maw of the Portal widened further and drooped down like a heavy-headed flower on a weakening stem. A blast of ferocious wind slammed against our barrier and rocked us all back on our heels. Inside the barrier, a cloud of foul-looking gas burst from the maw. Mike frantically cranked the van window shut again. The Pilgrims, the ones still alert and moving anyway, took up their chant again, many of them wailing and pounding on the barrier.

Rakow took one look at David who was shaking. Tears were running down his cheeks. I could feel it through our connection. All our strength was engaged, even with the help of the Guardian and the Coven, we were barely able to hold the amount of energy that was flying around the portal intact. If we broke, it was all over.

Rakow reached up to Becky who levitated him up behind her on the broom, just as neatly as an adult might pull a child up behind her on a horse. Rakow put both arms around her waist and said, "Go!" Becky circled around and clutched the chunk of meteor in her hand, chanting a spell. She circled around and prepared to make a run for it.

The maw of the Portal burst open wide and giant white snowflakes began to fall. Somehow, they made it almost all the way to the ground before the lava burned them up. I could see Mike and Jim through the pock-marked windshield, looking up in wonder, Jim at the Portal, Mike at the snow. Mike looked entirely at peace. Jim looked crazier than a shithouse rat. Jim seized a short staff, similar to the ones the cloaked Pilgrims all carried, and smashed out the windshield. Coughing and retching from the tainted air, he leaned forward over the dashboard, his arms spread, out the front of the van. Mike held him steady.

I looked at Becky and Rakow for what I feared was the last time. Anguish rushed through David, through Jen, through me. We all cried out in one voice, "No!"

Mike looked at David, his face full of love and said something, I couldn't tell what.

Just then, from out of nowhere, my mom appeared just a few feet to Becky's left! She was holding a weapon of some kind; I could hardly see what. The exertion of holding the wall around the Portal was so great, blood vessels were bursting in my eyes. Tears ran down, mixed with blood. David's heartbreak filled me.

My mom cocked one arm and released, and I realized what her weapon was. A toy slingshot. I recognized it. It was an old thing of Jon's that had been sitting in the garage on a shelf with a bunch of other toys slated for the next summer's garage sale. Lorraine had found it when she'd organized the basement last fall and slated it for removal.

I flashed back to Jen's vision from earlier in the night. *Slings and arrows* she'd said. Where had Mom been? I thought she'd been paying attention to Jim coming inside and then Maka, but she must have heard her. She must have known.

The stone she'd loaded in looked too polished and perfect to be just any stone, too. I recalled a basket full of polished quartz sitting on that same shelf, waiting their turn for the next summer's crafts. The stones would have been blessed already, I thought. Blessed by the whole Coven, like they did each new moon for the things they were preparing to sell. Rose quartz, I'd wager. A healing stone.

The stone flew true. It struck Becky just above her left ear, not hard enough to knock her out, but hard enough to disrupt her aim and make her dip the nose of her broom earthward.

The dogs took over from there. Tati hit her first. That leap, the one she'd practiced so many times with David. She leapt up and tangled herself into Becky's arms, forcing the broom further downwards. Alesta hit the broom from the rear, catching hold of the bristles with her teeth and hanging briefly midair before the broom fell low enough that her paws touched the ground. Shadow was last but far from least. He barreled full force at Rakow, all 97 pounds of ferocious German Shepherd, knocking his chosen human down off the broom and pinning him to the ground.

I felt David's rush of relief along with Jen's and my

own and then the maw of the Portal swung down and sucked the van up with a wrenching shriek of bending, melting metal. Jim hung on to the frame of the windshield, howling and crying up at the vast blackness inside the mouth of the Portal. Up they were drawn, up higher and higher. The Portal's mouth drew in on itself crushing the van like a dishrag. Then something reached through and wrenched the hole open again. Something from the other side.

Something or someone?

Through the pink haze of my vision, I swear I saw a hand reach down through the portal. A big hand, made of starlight and snow. It flicked open the drivers' side door of the van. The door fell crashing down and splashed into the pool of lava that was still happily broiling the little patch of previously fertile Nebraska soil that used to be grass and flowers.

The hand, if that's really what it was, stretched out and ever so gracefully and gently caught Mike in its palm as he tumbled out of the van. It delicately closed around him and drew him up and away. I don't think Jim even noticed, he only had eyes for the blackness that was consuming him, along with the Chevy Astro van. And then in a giant upward draft, the van door, the boulders, the bones and shards of volcanic glass, everything the wormhole had spit out of the Portal over the last few hours of its existence was sucked upwards. The Portal drew it all up and sucked it in to itself. The tiny, brilliant black hole became tinier and tinier and brighter and brighter until with an ear bending POP! It was gone.

Jen, David and I held it together for another maybe five seconds before we collapsed. The magical energy coming from the Coven sputtered and died. The only thing left at the end was the light from the Guardian's hands, held up above his head. Then it faded and he too fell to his knees and collapsed in exhaustion and the last barrier from around the Portal fell.

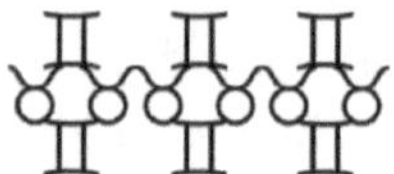

MR. RAKOW BROKE his wrist and shoulder when he hit the ground with Shadow on top of him. David got to him first while Jen and I were still on the ground trying to catch our breath. I don't know how he even got his feet under him, but he must have. I watched them through a pinkish haze.

Mr. Rakow tried to sit up and flinched. David caught him around the waist and eased him back down so they were leaning against one another. He undid Mr. Rakow's face mask and gently removed it.

"I tried," Mr. Rakow said, his voice unsteady. Shock and pain were making him speak slowly. "I tried to save him."

David pulled his own facemask off and tossed it aside. His eyes were wet with tears.

"I know you did," he said in a husky voice. "And the dogs and I got in your way." He sniffed.

"Why'd you do it?" Rakow asked, sounding confused. "Why didn't you let me try?" He looked at David, honest puzzlement in his voice.

I knew he wouldn't have tried to save Mike if he hadn't been David's dad. It was just way too crazy dangerous. I knew Becky was just crazy enough to try it, but I knew it never would have worked. If they'd tried it, they would either have crashed at full speed into our boundary wall, or if by some miracle that stone would have let them pass through, they'd have gotten sucked up into the Portal. There just wasn't enough time. I knew it, and my mom sure as heck knew it. Looking at David's face, I understood that he knew it too.

"I couldn't," he started, and his breath hitched. He took a breath and tried again. "I couldn't lose you both." Shadow and Tati nosed their way in, Tati under David's arm and Shadow, carefully nuzzling Rakow's cheek until he was looking right at David.

"I couldn't lose you." David said.

Mr. Rakow wore an expression I don't think I'd ever seen him wear. Not when he talked about classic cars or telling us about that first steak dinner he had after he got stateside after Vietnam, or even when he looked at Shadow. I don't know if I've ever seen as much love in anybody's eyes as the way he looked at David just then.

He scrubbed at his eyes with the back of his uninjured hand and cleared his throat.

"And you never will," he said. Then he grinned his wry, crooked grin. "Now help me get up and drive me to the ER so they can see what kind of damage my fool dog and you did to my arm in the name of keeping me alive."

David put his arm around Mr. Rakow, careful not to touch the hurt side, and helped him to his feet with great care.

Jen had pulled her own face mask off and dragged herself over to where I lay. She leaned on one elbow and peered down at me, tapping my helmet with one long nail. I reached up and pulled it off. We took one another by the hands and pulled each other up to sitting positions.

"Slings and arrows, eh?" I asked.

"Your mom has a killer arm," she replied.

"Angels?" I asked, thinking of the hand that had

caught Mike and spirited him away.

She shrugged. "I don't know what else I'd call that, do you?"

I shook my head. "Where do you suppose Mike is now? Do you think he's okay?"

"I'm not sure, but it feels…right. It feels like what happened is what was supposed to happen." She rubbed at her neck like it hurt. It probably did. I was pretty sure every part of my body hurt but I was still to shook up to register it. "Whatever else Mike was, I think he was something special. Maybe something too special to belong here on Earth with the rest of us poor saps."

I pondered that for a second and then rubbed at my forehead.

"My brain hurts," I said. "Let's go check and see how everybody is, and then …" I trailed off, unsure of what I wanted to do next.

"Ice cream," Jen said resolutely. "There should be ice cream."

"I really like the way you think."

David came over then. Mom was carefully looking Mr. Rakow over. Shadow was standing by and I could hear ambulances approaching.

"Is it over?" David asked. "Like, is the Portal closed for good?"

Jen nodded firmly. "It is. Done and done." Our complex high-five sequence was dutifully performed.

I was sure it would sink in soon, but at the moment, I was feeling a little numb. All around us was destruction. Downed buildings, holes in the ground, literally scorched earth where the lava had been. Our folks were milling around, checking in on one another. The radio in my coverall headset was still buzzing with witches talking back and forth, getting first aid where it needed to be.

The cloaked Pilgrims who were still around were in various states of weeping, wailing, talking, arguing, and skittering away before they had to talk to the police who were now fully on the scene. Officer Yardley was talking to Dad and supervising the EMTs who were putting Mr. Rakow on a gurney. Concerned clusters of people in rainbow-hued clothing were proffering first aid to anyone who needed it.

And in the midst of it, I felt a sense of peace trying to claim me, that I wasn't totally sure I trusted. I looked at my friends. Our necklaces glowed, but very faintly.

I asked what I knew we were all thinking.

"What now?"

# EPILOGUE

In the immediate aftermath, despite the fact that he was physically still back at home, Jon provided us all with timely check-ins and status reports.

David accompanied Mom and Mr. Rakow to the hospital, along with Maka, who'd been badly injured in the fight with the Eridani. One of them had gotten hold of her and they'd struggled. In the fight, the Eridani had breached her armor and she'd taken a huge dose of venom before Barb and Malinowski could get the creature off her. EMTs put her on a stretcher and rushed her out of there immediately.

Mom rode in the ambulance with Maka, and by the time they arrived at the hospital, Maka was awake and speaking coherently with the nurses. I told Jon to make Mom drink some water and sit down for a few minutes before she brought anybody else back from the brink of death. He promised to try.

I had joined Jen and Deanne on the broad steps in front of the campus library, checking over our less severely wounded people. Between us, we were able to mend Ginny's cracked femur from when she was jolted off the bleachers by earthquake activity, and disenchant Rome's bespelled face from where one of the witches who breached the outer spell wall hit her with a frogface charm. Jon had to consult Phillida's book on that one. Then we unblackened Jules's black eye where she took a punch from an angry neighbor, meant for a skinny 17-year-old kid with pink hair, and listened while she called the neighbor creative and hilarious names which she immediately bespelled us never to repeat.

*Witches.*

I joke, but truly all the witches were suffering from some amount of shock that night. Elizabeth's right hand had clenched her magic pen for so long, she couldn't unclench it. The severe cramp was painful and it had spread to her right arm and chest. That was a weird one. When I reached out to her with my healing senses tuned in, what I touched felt like a super-concentrated panic attack. Deanne had to pitch in with me, to surround it with enough calming magic to get it to even begin to dissipate. It took a while, but it eventually worked.

Jon explained to me that once the barriers had come down, the Coven witches had to make their way in toward the center of campus harried by the various groups of Pilgrim witches they'd been holding off for hours, who were looking for payback.

This magical battle between witches added confusion and chaos to the already confused groups of neighborhood homeowners jolted out of their beds by the unusual activity outside, Pride activists there looking for the party Jim had invited them to attend, the ones who'd gotten a whiff of something miraculous that might be about to happen, and the few who were fully on board with Jim and his zealot Pilgrim friends. Then there were the Pilgrims themselves, who were wholly intent on jumping into the portal with Jim.

Those folks who wanted to but hadn't made it to the portal before it closed up had disappeared pretty quickly afterwards. That included most of the folks sporting cloaks, all the witches, and the two drag queens Dottie had spotted talking to Jim before he rammed the Astro van into the spell wall.

That left behind a lot of confused people with quite a

few minor injuries amongst the crowd remaining. After we'd excused Barb and Malinowski, who were completely unscathed and anxious to join Maka at the hospital, we took care of the Coven, and then joined the folks waiting to see the completely overwhelmed group of EMTs who'd arrived on scene. We held some hands and administered a few doses of my version of Mom's Vitamin L. The accompanying aroma of lavender was comforting, along with the citrusy scent of orange that seemed to accompany all my magic.

Nicole and Lisa came with us, pulling from a seemingly bottomless tote bag piles of small hand-knit blankets, just the right size to wrap around a cold, shocky person's shoulders and chock full of magic that made one feel very relaxed. So very relaxed that troublesome memories like falling down into a bottomless pit or being chased by a bonfire with legs seem only mildly amusing instead of trauma inducing.

Jen paused abruptly for a moment, then turned to me. "Something's up with Becky. I need to go talk to mom and Dottie," she said.

"Is she okay?" I asked, anxiously.

"She will be," answered Jen confidently.

The balanced health of all the Coven members was always of paramount importance to Lorraine and Dot. The Coven witches were a powerful bunch that needed thoughtful and wise leaders to care for them in moments when they might not be able to care for themselves. Pat checked in with them first, before disappearing abruptly, as was her custom, but I hadn't seen Becky since we'd looked at the lump on her head my mom had given her to keep her from her ill planned if well meant plan to rescue Mike.

For the moment, at least, the others seemed to me to

be doing pretty normal, healthy things. Diane and Jules were already lurking around the ground damaged by the portal, and especially the lava, and beginning the work of healing the ground. Ginny, Rome and Charlotte were having an animated conversation with a group of terrifically fit firefighters that looked to me to be the beginning of several lovely friendships, at least for a while.

In a similar vein, Elizabeth was swarmed by a pair of young women in brightly colored t-shirts with many ear and a few nose piercings, who seemed a bit starstruck by what they believed they'd seen her do that night. She seemed to find them interesting. Like most supernatural things, different people perceive magic different ways when they see it. Mostly, they don't see it. Some folks do. The three of them wandered off, talking.

Just then, Becky turned up. Lisa, Nicole and Deanne surrounded her and listened as Becky alternated between vehement protestations that she could have made it through, that she might have been able to save Mike, crying jags, and despondent silence. Lorainne and Dottie joined them and gently herded them back towards their vehicles while organizing safe transportation back to Lisa and Nicole's house where all of them were instructed to go, together, and get some food and rest.

It was almost 4 a.m. when Jen finally dropped me off at my house and took herself off to her bed. Mom was home, but Dad was still back on campus, being available to the police and making sure that everyone understood that they should be looking to the underground utilities on campus for a reason why two buildings had collapsed and one area of campus seemed to have been burned or melted by something very hot. Natural gas, he suggested. Look to the campus power plant. The folks reporting bottomless pits and lava on campus? Well, they had been at a party, and there was quite likely some drinking going on. Pretty hard to take that sort of thing seriously, you know?

There was remarkably little blowback about the whole thing. Officer Yardley was, of course, instrumental in that. In fact, all across the board, things got pretty quiet after the portal closed. Rakow was home by breakfast, in a shoulder brace instead of a cast, thanks to my mom's early intervention. Maka was home within a couple of days, and she, much to Barb's and Malinowski's relief, bowed to my mom's request that she not go off planet for at least several weeks, ideally months.

Then, you know, there was school. There was the spring play, and of course, Prom, which we all went to totally on the grounds that this was our last chance at one. Not like we were at all interested in dressing up and going out to dinner someplace with tablecloths, or at least actual silverware. Then a dance with our sweeties? Nah. Total snooze.

Before we knew it, we were getting ready for graduation, and still, the hinky side of our world remained quiet. No critters, no trolls, no ghosts, no missing kids, no aliens, no nothing. It was beginning to make me edgy.

I caught Dad at breakfast one Saturday morning and quizzed him about it.

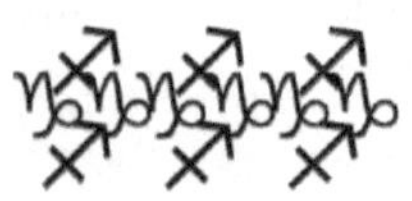

"WHAT DO YOU think is going on around here?" I asked as he shuffled in wrapped in a bathrobe, his hair askew. "We haven't had a single report of trouble since the night the portal closed. I've been searching Phyllida's book, and I'm finding nothing. What's the deal?" I asked, shoving the creamer closer to him as he poured himself coffee.

He made me wait for his answer. He sat down and had his first sip of coffee. Then he snagged the toast bread from the bottom shelf of the 1960s-era metal kitchen cart that their 1960s-era vintage toaster had sat upon for the last three decades, and would sit upon for at least three more. He drew out two slices of wheat bread, dropped them in the toaster and pushed the lever down.

"It turns out, I may know something about that. I talked to Maka and Bernard last night." He said, preparing the butter and jam for his toast.

"Yeah?" I asked, trying not to snort-laugh. Malinowski's first name never failed to crack me up. Dad quirked an eyebrow at me and smiled. He knew it too.

"They've been going back over their journals and archives while Maka's been recuperating. They've noticed a similar pattern in two of the other places they know of where a Portal has closed in a populated area. Afterwards, there's been a notable period of calm."

"Here's what's interesting, too. It's not just a calm of supernatural energies, but also whatever life forms are in that particular space. Less trouble. More peace talks. Even the weather seems to cooperate. Bumper crops are recorded in following years. Birth rates go up. Life thrives." His toast popped up and he snagged it gingerly.

"Really?" I asked. That was pretty cool, and then my inner Mr. Rakow piped up. "For how long?" I asked, and waited for the other shoe to drop.

"Excellent question, kiddo," Dad said. "From what they've been able to piece together, the effect doesn't seem to last more than four or five decades, tops." He smiled broadly then took a big bite of toast.

*Oh!*

"You mean, we might actually get some time off from hunting baddies?" I asked, trying to gather together all the threads of what a lull might mean.

"I don't think we should stop paying attention, of course, but it sure does seem like we all might be able to take a bit of a breather," he said, smiling.

I looked at him carefully. He'd had this burden on his shoulders for years, since before I was born. He must be exhausted. His face had wrinkles, plenty of the smiley kind around his eyes, but plenty of the frowny ones between his brows as well. His hair was definitely grayer than it had been since the last time I paid any attention to it.

And then I thought about college. I'd been planning to attend the University of Nebraska, right here in Lincoln. I'd felt obligated to stick close, knowing that David, Jen and I would be guarding the Portal, and protecting our hometown.

But, what if I didn't have to?

I mean, I'd sent out applications to a couple of my dream colleges, just sort of for fun, to see if I might get accepted. And I had. To all the ones I'd applied to. Up to and including Radcliffe, with a generous scholarship offer.

What if?

I looked up at Dad, wide eyed. He smiled back at me broadly and raised his coffee cup.

What if?

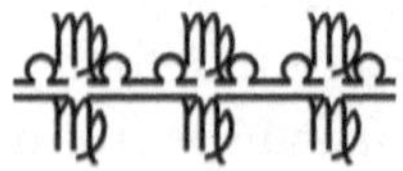

THAT VERY AFTERNOON, Barb and Malinowski surprised us all by announcing their engagement. Since neither one of them had even a drop of traditional wedding planning blood in their veins, I suspected this was a ploy to keep Maka distracted and planet-bound for another month. She, like Rakow, was having some residual heart difficulties from the Eridani venom. She, like Rakow, was disinclined to listen to anyone telling them they couldn't do something.

So, a wedding it was to be. Honestly, I couldn't wait. I was dying to see what kind of fabulously cool ceremonial trappings they would use from their wildly adventurous lives. I'd need to enchant a couple of nice-looking notebooks for the occasion.

And in the pell-mell turmoil of the next thirty days, amidst the wedding preparations, we thought about the future. That is to say, we *all* did. Once we'd come to the conclusion that staying in Lincoln was optional, the three of us were *bombarded* with suggestions from our elders as to what exactly we needed to be doing with ourselves.

Two nights before the wedding, I sent Jen and David beeper messages to meet up at The Mill, downtown at nine. It was a local coffee shop in an old part of town trying to be new and hip. They did a fine job of it.

I got there early and snagged a table by the bookshelves. I sat and watched people walk down the street outside. It was mid-July and stupid hot out. My stress level had been mounting for weeks. College admissions deadlines were looming. There was a possible internship, and a scholarship with an expiration date, ugh. The coffee, conversely, calmed me.

Between the tables and the window sat a telescope. Hard telling what it was supposed to be looking at, as the folks at the table next to me had done their level best to screw up any settings it may have once had. I was glad to see them packing up as David and Jen walked inside together.

I had watched them from the moment the met outside at the corner. The effortlessly complex series of high-five maneuvers. The shoulder-to-shoulder walk, punctuated by a full stop, some piece of animated conversation, followed by Jen's full laugh and David's triumphant smile. Making us laugh is like an Olympic sport for him, and he relishes the win.

Jen came in first, facing the barista, but pointing one long red fingernail directly at me over in the corner by the books. David, right behind her, took her cue and came my way. He pulled up a chair and flopped down, grinning.

"Why are you so smiley?" I asked.

"Jen got one of her good vibes about this conversation on her way over here," he said. "I'm all in for Jen's good vibes!" He jumped up and briefly examined the bookshelf on the wall beside us, then turned back and leaned over the back of a chair, tapping out some complicated rhythm with his fingers on the table.

Jen approached with a coffee in one hand, a plate with a cinnamon roll in the other, and a can of soda tucked under her arm. David relieved her of his soda. He tried to take the roll, too, but she pulled it away.

She sat down, settled herself and her things comfortably, then looked at me.

"Talk."

"Well, you know I was kinda leaning towards school instead of the Internship," I said.

"Right," David said. "But then you were kicking yourself because the internship had travel, and you want to travel."

"But you didn't like the way the Internship was structured, or that Supervisor, who was awful," Jen reminded me.

"Right, exactly." I took a sip of my coffee and set it down. "So, then I'm ready to commit to Radcliffe, and then I got this last-minute offer."

"From who?" Jen asked, pointedly.

"From Dottie!" I said, nervously. "She's been planning a trip abroad. She's slated to do some research for a new book she's writing about Mesopotamian art. But she hadn't planned to go alone. She had a research assistant lined up, who ended up breaking both legs in a car accident yesterday and isn't going anyplace for a while."

"Bummer," David interjected, looking longingly at Jen's cinnamon roll. She ignored him. I continued.

"Dot has all the travel plans already booked and paid for the two of them. They planned to travel all around Iraq and Syria, with side trips for conferences in Egypt and Greece. She needs someone who can act as her research assistant, which I can totally do, and just general travel assistant, which I know absolutely nothing about. I've never organized anything beyond a trip to the movie theater!"

"That's not true," David said, frowning. "You're the one that mapped out the routes that Troll was using and figured out how we could block him in and end his reign of terror on the Belmont neighborhood pets. You had to go explore a bunch of places you'd never been before and figure out how they all connected."

"Well, yeah," I said slowly.

"And we all know any plan is only as good as first contact. The real trick is being able to adapt to the situation and accomplish the mission," Jen reminded me.

"That's true!" I said, feeling more hopeful than I had

in hours. It was a crazy good opportunity to travel with someone my parents and I both totally trusted. "I'd be expected to journal extensively, of course, to make it all a genuine learning experience in the eyes of my folks and higher education, but that's not a problem."

"How long would you be gone?" David asked.

"That's another thing," I said, my tummy clenching again. "Dottie has plans booked out for the next nine months, and she said it wouldn't surprise her if it ended up taking a year!"

Jen smiled at me. "You're gonna do it, aren't you?"

And suddenly, I was quite sure that I was. No more worrying about making the right decisions. No debilitating nervousness.

"Yes! I'm going to tell her yes!" I declared.

"All right!" David crowed. Our hands met over the table, the classic high five with wiggle fingers to celebrate the explosive good news.

Jen grinned too, but then she stood and walked over to the bookshelf.

"What is it, Jen?" I asked.

She turned to face me. "How do you feel about being away from Jon for that long?" It was a blunt question, but it was said in an objective way, like Jen was trying to put together the pieces of a puzzle only she could see.

"We've talked about it a bunch," I said. "Like, all different ways of being apart, either at school or job or whatever. I know Lorraine was trying to figure out some family trips for you guys too. I'm sorry, I've had my head buried in this since yesterday afternoon, are there any updates for you guys?"

"Yeah," she said cautiously. I perked up.

"Yeah?" I asked.

"So, we're a for sure visiting my grandma on Dad's

side from August to the end of October. I think we'll probably take off before the snow falls, though. I'm okay with living without all the conveniences in hot weather, but I think my modern sensibilities may draw the line at zero degrees Fahrenheit."

Lorraine said their grandma on that side lived a very traditional life on a reservation north of us. Their Dad said she was stubborn and pig headed and insisted on living back of beyond. The plan was to stay out there with her for an extended time to learn more about their ancestors.

"Cool!" I said, then I paused. "Is there more?" I asked.

"Yeah. Maka is planning another trip off planet. Between our moms, Barb, and Malinowski, they've kept her here recuperating for as long as they could, but she's bound and determined to go before Winter solstice. There's a once in a millennia planetary conjunction she wants to get a closer look at, and she wants me and Jon to go with her. In fact, she's insisting, and I feel strongly that it's important that we go."

In other words, her prophetic powers were nudging her in this direction. Strongly, from the sound of it.

"Cool, which planets?" I asked, thinking back to our adventure to visit Callean, and the amazing view we'd been able to see of our solar system.

"Well, we don't exactly have names for them, just numbers." Jen replied.

*Crap*

"How far away does she want to go?" I asked, slowly.

"Just to Alpha Centauri," Jen replied slowly.

Oh, sure. Okay. Just the next solar system over. Yikes. I took a breath and tried to rein in my initial reaction, which was to completely overthink this. I had no worries whatsoever about Jon's and my ability to be instantly in touch anywhere on earth. I hadn't really thought through what it might mean to be separated from him and Jen, by a distance measured in light years, I had no idea if Jon's ability to *piggyback* into my mind or the connection with Jen through our living stone necklaces would work from that distance. We wouldn't know until we tried.

"For how long?" David asked.

"She wants to be back here by the end of next summer at the latest, she says. There's some event coming up in Germany she wants to attend in person, around the end of September or the beginning of October, and she wants some down time to prepare.

I chewed on that. It meant David and I might go months without any contact with Jon and Jen at all. I would worry, I was sure of that. Not unduly, I supposed, since they'd be with Lorraine and Maka, but still. I was used to talking to Jon multiple times a day, easily as much as I talked to Jen. Not having those connections would stink, if it happened. I stood and fiddled with the telescope, wondering where Alpha Centauri was in the sky right now.

"Are Barb and Malinowski going too?" David asked.

Jen smiled. "They were planning to, but that's about to change," she said, winking and tapping her forehead with one finger.

"What's about to change?" He asked.

"I have a very strong hunch they're going to be busy with a new baby by winter solstice," Jen exclaimed.

"Oh my gosh!" I cried. "That's so great!" I scooted back up to the table where Jen had resumed her seat, and started cutting her cinnamon roll into three pieces.

"If I'm right, they're going to announce it tomorrow night at dinner, so act surprised, you two!"

David pantomimed zipping his lip. I did the same.

"What about you, David?" Jen asked. "You and Rakow have been thick as thieves for weeks. What are you two cooking up?"

"If it all works out, I think we'll be travelling too. Mr. Rakow has a line on a camper van. If he can swing it, we're thinking of packing up the dogs and heading west. He's got some places in mind in Colorado, then up through Wyoming and Montana, out to the coast, then even further north. He has an old army buddy living in British Columbia who has a martial arts school. Mr. Rakow seems to think it would be good for both of us to study with her for a while."

I swear, it was like a light bulb went off over Jen's head. Her whole face lit up.

"That's it!" She exclaimed. "That's almost the last part falling into place." She carefully placed two pieces of cinnamon roll onto two napkins and handed one to each of us. "Look, this is going to be a good year for all of us. I can already tell, but there's one more thing we need to do before we leave here tonight."

"What is it?" I asked, picking up on her excitement.

"Bring on the mojo," David grinned.

"We need to agree to meet back here a year from to-day. We have to make the pact. We need to swear by the stones," she said.

I could already feel the familiar warmth near my col-larbone. The faint blue light shone through my white t-shirt, seeking out Jen's red and David's green stones. We joined hands and shared a happy look. Jen spoke.

"By the grace of our ancestors, let our adventures be many, our mishaps be few, and let us be well until we meet again, one year hence in this very place," she murmured quietly under the hum of conversation from nearby tables.

"So mote it be," I whispered, calling forth a little blast of my healing magic to share with my friends.

"Speak those words of wisdom," David said, drawing on the magic of Lennon and McCartney. "Let it be."

I heard a single distant drumbeat, and then the scent of orange blossoms and the sweet sound of a C chord on the piano filled the air around us. We proceeded to stuff ourselves with cinnamon roll and talk and laugh for another hour, enjoying the time we had together, here and now.

# The Zodiac Cusp Kids

**♍︎♎ Angie Parsons** 9/22/70 - Cusp of Beauty (Virgo/Libra) Musician, scholar. Necklace - blue. Dating Jon.

**♉︎♊ David Owens** 5/20/70 - Cusp of Energy (Taurus/Gemini) Athlete - football, then cross country after losing an eye in battle with Mitch. Necklace - green.

**♐︎♑ Jen Howe** 12/21/69 - Cusp of Prophecy (Sagittarius/Capricorn) Twin sister to Jon. Actor in school theater productions. Has prophetic visions.

# The Family

**♐︎♑ Jon Howe** 12/21/1969 - Cusp of Prophecy (Sagittarius/Capricorn) Developing psychic 'sight' while losing his everyday sight. Twin brother to Jen. Dating Angie.

**♊︎♋ Lorraine Howe** Cusp of Magic (Gemini/Cancer) Jen and Jon's mom. Coven leader.

**♒︎♓ Professor Alden Parsons** Cusp of Sensitivity (Aquarius/Pisces) - Angie's dad. The Guardian.

**♌︎♍ Elizabeth Parsons** Cusp of Exposure (Leo/Virgo) - Angie's mom.

**♎ Mallory Parsons** Angie's older sister.

**♋ Donna Owens** David's mom. In car accident with Mitch (Something Wicked) and suffered traumatic brain injury. Never recovered completely & lived in nursing home. Was possessed by Jeanne's magic (Something Twisted) which ultimately led to her passing.

# Fellow Adventurers

**Mr. Rakow** — Vietnam veteran. Neighbor to David's mom, Donna. Friend to Lorraine and the Parsons.

**Maka (The Grandmother)** — Advisor to Lorrain, Rakow and the Parsons. Powerful magic user.

**Malinowski** — Orphaned in an attack on his moon. Rescued by and is companion/journeyman to Maka (Something Found.) In a relationship with Barb.

**Barb** — Troubled kid, living in group home at Whitehall. Got involved with the Zodiac Cusp Kids when her friend's sister was kidnapped. Taken on as apprentice to Maka after the events of Something Lost. In a relationship with Malinowski.

# The Coven

**Shelly** — Grew up in Lincoln. Returned after college to care for aging mother. Ex-bf is Viktor. Best friends with Miss Charlotte. Dog: Tati. Magic color: Deep rose.

**Lisa** — Local to Nebraska. Family owns much land and invested well. Teaches ad hoc classes at the University. Apprenticed to Maka. Knits constantly. Adept with abundance spells. Expert at amplifying spell intensity. Girlfriend: Nicole. Magic Color: wheat gold.

**Nicole** — Originally from Salem, Mass. Recently changed jobs from the University Library to the Public Library - filled the opening left by Jeanne's exit in Something Twisted. Current Girlfriend: Lisa. Ex-girlfriend: Pat. Working with Elizabeth on managing familiars. Expert at Rune magic. Magic color: ocean blue.

♈ Rome  Originally from Kansas. Assistant Manager
at local retro diner. Fabric designer and
seamstress. Dates Michael, a biracial local
musician. Expert at designing spells, works
with Deanne and Lisa to craft new spells for
the Coven. Magic color: Fuchsia

♓ Deanne  Local to Nebraska. Works as archivist at
the local newspaper. Emotional caretaker
of the coven. Rescues troubled cats. Expert
at grasping the potential complexities of
new spell creation. Has some empathic
abilities, enhanced by magic. Magic color:
sky blue

♒ Becky  Recently graduated high school. Plays
drums in the punk band, Skurge Puppies.
Was observed by Dottie shoplifting using
magic. Was given help and training from
the Coven on controlling her use of magic.
Expert at sensory magic, including
invisibility spells. Magic color: deep blue

♏ Elizabeth  Junior at UNL studying anthropology and
political science. Aspiring novelist. Expert
at working with complex, many-stage
spells. Adept at working with familiars,
particularly cats. Magic color: deep purple

♊ Diane  Master Gardiner, has an acreage outside of
town where she's curated a large fenced
prairie garden. Also has a farm near
Lawrence, KS. Expert at working with
botanical magics. Three dogs: Bailey, Jim
and Huck. Magic color: forest green

♐ Ginny  Young mom of three. Lives with her mother
who taught her magic. Adept at working
with creative energies. Animal lover - de
facto home to all neighborhood strays.
Expert at multiplying power across
members of the spellcasting group.
Boyfriend: Chuck. Magic color: new leaf
green

♊ Jules   PhD student, frequent traveler, part time scientist. Adept at micro magic - spells that exerted tiny changes at critical levels in a system. Expert at identifying and working with stones to assist in working the Coven's magic. Boyfriend: Aurthur. Magic color: sun-blasted sand

♑ Dottie   Oldest coven member. Retired Art--History professor. Friends with Angie's dad and Shelly's mom. Adept at group magic. Expert at detecting tiny flaws capable of derailing destructive magic spells. Magic color: pure silver

♌ Pat   Nicole's ex. PhD student in Genetics. Bartender at a seedy downtown dive. Adept at detecting concealment spells. Expert at digging up long lost spells and lore. Magic color: grey/black

# The Pack

Shadow   German Shepherd. He/him. Human: Mr. Rakow

Bast   Siamese. HRH. Human: Answers to no one. Sometimes chooses to look after Angie

Tati   Yellow English Lab. She/her. Human: Shelly

Alesta   German Shepherd. She/her. Human: Barb

Bailey, Jim and Huck   English Shepherds. Bailey: she/her, Jim & Huck: he/him Human: Diane

Smokey   Cat. Gray/brown tabby. He/him. Human: Charlotte

# The Neighborhood

**Officer Yardley** — Neighborhood Lincoln Police Department officer. Can also see some of the things Mr. Rakow and the Zodiac Cusp Kids see. Assists in most cases where anything hinky might be going on. Slayed Great Dane-sized spiders at the mall with Mr. Rakow in *Something Twisted*

**Miss Jeanne** — Former Wesleyan student of Professor Parsons. Former librarian at the neighborhood branch. Disappears after the events of *Something Twisted*.

**Miss Charlotte** — Downtown Librarian. Has worked with Angie often on research projects. Best friends with Shelly. Cat: Smokey

**Clint** — Jen's 1971 Brown Chevy Impala. Seatbelts for six. Theoretical space for nine.

# Trouble

**Viktor** — Shelly's ex-boyfriend. History of stalking.

**Arthur** — Jules's boyfriend. Drives a Trans-Am.

**Chuck** — Ginny's boyfriend. Breeds dogs. Drives a truck. Regular at Rome's diner

**Siouxzy** — Former in-home health aide to Shelly's mom.

**Mike** — David's dad. Left Lincoln for California before David was born. Road manager for the band, Lucid Absurdity. AIDS activist. Inorog?

**Jim** — Mike's friend. Lead singer for Lucid Absurdity. AIDS activist

# Tales of the

# Zodiac Cusp Kids

Available from Snowy Wings Publishing

# Something Wicked
the First Tale of the Zodiac Cusp Kids

It's 1983. Angie, Jenny, and David are watching MTV, riding bikes, and looking forward to summer vaca-tion before they start junior high school. Lincoln, Ne-braska is a pretty quiet place to grow up, and when the kids take off at 5:00 am to deliver newspapers on Jenny's route, they aren't expecting trouble. So, when a creature straight out of a horror movie appears, the kids are forced to draw on their wits, their strengths, and most of all their friendship to survive.


# Something Haunted
the Second Tale of the Zodiac Cusp Kids

The summer of 1983 is over. After weeks of healing from their first adventure and some specialized basic training with Mr. Rakow, Angie, Jenny and David are feeling prepared for the horrors junior high will surely bring. The final weekend of vacation, a bizarre tornado tears through Lincoln, upending gravestones and depos-iting supernatural debris on the school grounds. The gang has their hands full with the demands of starting junior high on top of trying to figure out an otherworldly mystery, and their friendship begins to feel the strain. But the malevolent ghost haunting the school is ramping up its attacks on students, and the kids are going to have to get it together in time to save the school.

# Something Lost
### the Third Tale of the Zodiac Cusp Kids

It's a Friday afternoon in the spring of 1985, when Crystal and Barb, two girls from Whitehall, the neigh-borhood group home for troubled kids, approach Angie at school. Crystal's little sister has disappeared, and her foster parents and the police think she's just another runaway. Crystal doesn't believe it, and when she and Barb learn there's a ghost involved, they know they're going to need the kind of help Angie, David and Jenny have developed a reputation for. The Zodiac Cusp Kids enlist some extra help from Jen's twin Jon and a couple of very special German Shepherd pups to uncover what has really happened to Crystal's sister, and what they find is darker and more complex than anyone imagined.

# Something Found
### the Fourth Tale of the Zodiac Cusp Kids

Just over a week has passed since Angie, David and Jenny said goodbye to Barb and Alesta, the German Shepherd pup when David and Jenny convince Jon and Angie to come to a dance at the neighborhood Rec Cen-ter. Mysterious things begin to appear as soon as the girls start getting ready for the dance. Jenny's prophecies guide them to a magical artifact that transports the Zo-diac Cusp Kids away from the dance on a world-hopping rescue that opens their eyes to a terrifying new enemy, and to some powerful magical allies closer to home than they'd dreamed.

Something Found is the fourth of seven stories drawn from Angie's diaries. Kept safely hidden for dec-ades, they tell how the kids spent their teenage years – working with their mentor, Mr. Rakow, and Jenny's mom, Lorraine, who dabbles in witchcraft, to realize their power and battle the forces of darkness that men-ace their hometown.

# Something Twisted

### the Fifth Tale of the Zodiac Cusp Kids

Two years have passed since Angie, David, and Jenny returned from their star-hopping adventure and learned the identity of the Guardian. Now sophomores in high school, the kids are trying to juggle saving their hometown while also having social lives, playing on sports teams, acting in plays, and studying healing magic outside of class. When those worlds begin to collide with dangerous magic, the kids have their hands full figuring out who to trust. Then, David's mom gets dragged into the mess and the Guardian puts his relationship with the whole team on the line to discover the identity of the culprit. Plus, Great Dane-sized-spiders. Hold onto your hats, Something Twisted is going on!

# Something Fatal

### the Sixth Tale of the Zodiac Cusp Kids

1987 is a rough year for Angie, David and Jen. Just weeks after the tragic passing of David's mom, one of the members of Lorraine's coven goes missing. Untan-gling the web of lies, thievery and intrigue surrounding her misadventure is a challenge fit for Agatha Christie. Unless Angie and the others can figure out who is re-sponsible for Shelly's death, the emotional and magical well-being of the entire Coven is at risk, and that bodes ill for everyone in the state of Nebraska and beyond.

# Something Final

## the Last Tale of the Zodiac Cusp Kids

The adventures of the Zodiac Cusp Kids are laid to rest in the raw, cold February of 1989. The Portal has been spilling out more goop and increasingly dangerous goons for the past two years, and it's getting worse. On top of that, the kids are facing a mysterious and charis-matic figure from David's past who's not sitting quite right with Jenny. In order to decode the symbols from her vision, there's only one thing to do; a week-long cram session at the library. The things they discover lead them straight toward the fight of everyone's lives. It's going to take every trick they've learned and the com-bined powers of The Coven, The Guardian, and the Zo-diac Cusp Kids to end this story. Something Final is the last of the stories drawn from Angie's diaries. Kept safely hidden for decades, they tell how the kids spent their teenage years - working with their mentor, Mr. Rakow, and Jenny's mom, Lorraine, who leads a coven, to come to the life-changing conclu-sion of their journey together.

# About the Author

Sarah Dale is an author, mom, partner, daughter, step-mom, friend, dog-walker, cat-appreciator, library book-balancer, word lover, think-thinker and picture-taker living in Lincoln, Nebraska, and just generally trying to get things done.

www.sarahdaleauthor.com

Facebook: facebook.com/wecouldbeheroesnovel/

Twitter: @sarahdaleauthor

Instagram: instagram.com/wecouldbeheroesnovel/

Goodreads: goodreads.com/stillphoenix

Amazon: amazon.com/author/stillphoenix

# Other titles you might enjoy from Snowy Wings Publishing

*Thelma Bee in Toil and Treble*
- Erin Petti.
https://www.snowywingspublishing.com/book/thelma-
bee-in-toil-and-treble/


*A Darkness at the Door*
- Intisar Khanani
https://www.snowywingspublishing.com/book/a-dark-
ness-at-the-door/


*Time Bound*
- Micky O'Brady
https://www.snowywingspublishing.com/book/time-
bound/

www.ingramcontent.com/pod-product-compliance
Lightning Source LLC
Chambersburg PA
CBHW031026190726

48286CB00003BA/1044